'There's nothing I can do to change my grand-mother's ludicrous will—but there's a hell of a lot I can do to minimise its effect. Getting you out of my house won't present too many problems and neither, I hope, will getting you out of my business——'

'*Your* house—*your* business?' cut in Jane, shaking with anger. 'I own fifty per cent of both, and you'll get me out of neither!'

'Oh, no?' he murmured softly, his eyes glittering chips of ice as they held hers. 'As I've already pointed out, it's inevitable that we shall have an affair. . .the strong sexual attraction between us is something I intend exploiting to the full. It's when that affair has run its course that you will move out of my house. . .and you'll do so simply because your pride won't let you remain once I've lost interest in you. Though how long that will take—my losing interest, that is—we have yet to find out.'

CONTRACT TO LOVE

BY
KATE PROCTOR

MILLS & BOON LIMITED
ETON HOUSE   18–24 PARADISE ROAD
RICHMOND   SURREY   TW9 1SR

First published in Great Britain 1991
by Mills & Boon Limited

© Kate Proctor 1991

Australian copyright 1991
Philippine copyright 1991
This edition 1991

ISBN 0 263 77298 5

Set in 10 on 11 pt Linotron Palatino
01-9111-55184
Typeset in Great Britain by Centracet, Cambridge
Made and printed in Great Britain

CHAPTER ONE

DANIEL BLAKE was an angry man. His anger was manifested in the clenched set of aggressively handsome features and in the barely perceptible tic working sporadically on the cheek in Jane Ashford's line of vision.

Oh, yes, Daniel Blake was undoubtedly a very angry man, Jane decided—though remarkably restrainedly so, given the rumours she had heard of the explosive quality of his temper.

She was having no difficulty in judging Daniel Blake's reaction to the words being uttered by Marcus Watson, the elderly solicitor now disclosing the contents of the late Dolly Blake's will, Jane realised uncomfortably, but defining her own was an altogether different matter.

Composing the gentle loveliness of her features into a look of frowning concentration, though still half convinced she was dreaming, she forced her attention back to those soporific words her mind was having such difficulty accepting.

'In addition to my fifty per cent holding in Blake Enterprises, I have also, after considerable soul-searching, decided that my half-share in the Windsor Gardens house shall go to Joe Marley's sole surviving heir—the said Miss Jane Marley,' continued the solicitor. 'I realise that this decision will be regarded with as much antipathy by my grandson, Daniel Blake, as will be the disposal of my share of the business. . .' Marcus Watson broke off to allow the explosive manifestation of Daniel Blake's antipathy to abate. 'But I hope he will better understand my

5

reasons for both actions once he has read the letter he will shortly receive.'

One look at Daniel Blake's scowling features told Jane that Dolly Blake had either been a fool or an incurable optimist to hope her grandson would ever understand these plainly bizarre bequests of hers.

Forcing her attention back to the solicitor's continuing words, Jane heard confirmed one of her late grandfather's many claims in his occasional ranting tirades against his erstwhile partner, Robert Blake—that the house in the prestigious Windsor Gardens had once been his.

'Miss Ashford, I wonder if I might have a word with you,' murmured Marcus Watson, approaching her as the beneficiaries of Dolly Blake's will began drifting out of the wood-panelled room more usually set aside for board of directors' meetings.

Jane gazed up at the elderly man now at her side, flicking behind her ears, in a gesture of nervous reflex, the fine curtain of dark blonde hair falling forwards against her cheeks.

'Yes, I. . . I'm sorry,' she stammered, wanting to rise but unwilling to trust her legs as she caught sight of Daniel Blake striding towards them. 'I'm afraid my mind's simply refusing to take any of this in.'

'That's more than understandable,' sympathised the solicitor, turning slightly as Daniel Blake, a chillingly grim set to his strikingly handsome features, reached them.

'My legal people will be in touch with you,' he informed Marcus Watson tersely.

The solicitor nodded, his face impassive as he handed him an envelope. 'The letter to which your grandmother referred,' he explained.

Without a word, Daniel Blake accepted the envelope, a glacial sharpness in the blue of his luxuriantly lashed eyes as they swept perfunctorily over Jane's slim, still-seated figure.

'I shall be in my office when you've finished here, Miss Ashford. . .or perhaps now you intend reverting to Miss Marley?' he enquired icily, then turned and left.

'I'm afraid my advice to the late Mrs Blake—to pre-warn both you and her grandson—fell on deaf ears,' sighed Marcus Watson, taking the seat beside Jane's and depositing his file on the highly polished surface of the table before them. 'Not having met you, she felt it better that I should explain her actions to you, rather than writing to you as she did her grandson. . .though I must point out that Mrs Blake chose only to tell me the barest bones of the facts.'

Jane said nothing; she was still waiting in vain for her mind to waver in its conviction this was all a dream.

'I take it you do know something of the Blake-Marley feud?' asked the solicitor, his tone expressing mild alarm.

Jane's wide-spaced blue eyes darkened with reflex recoil. Because of that feud her grandfather had ended up financially ruined and, in his later years, was given to sporadic outpourings of demented recrimination: but the bitterness had eaten away at her father until it had ultimately destroyed his marriage to her mother and left him a stranger to his only daughter. And now she was being asked if she knew anything of the cause of the backlash that could so easily have destroyed her life!

'I know that my grandfather and Robert Blake had been business partners and that Robert Blake cheated him out of all he possessed,' she said tonelessly.

'I may not be in possession of all the details, but I can assure you it wasn't as cut and dried as that,' stated Marcus Watson gently. 'From what I know, one was as big a rogue as the other. . .even my late client was prepared to admit that.' He hesitated slightly before continuing. 'Were you aware that your grandfather and the late Mrs Blake had once been engaged to be married?'

Jane shook her head, unable to hide her astonishment.

'Though the eventual disintegration—for want of a better word—of the business partnership took place many, many years later, my late client gave me to understand that the root of it, and all the ensuing bitterness, lay to a large extent in her breaking off her engagement to your grandfather and in her subsequent marriage to Robert Blake.'

'Did she give you any details?'

He shook his head. 'Perhaps her letter to her grandson contains more than she disclosed to me.'

Jane shrugged. 'So it all boils down to *cherchez la femme*,' she murmured with a touch of bitterness. 'And Dolly Blake decided to salve her conscience through me.'

Both the chuckle the man gave and its undisguised warmth surprised Jane.

'I doubt if you'd have made that statement had you known Mrs Blake. Guilt was not a burden she carried, but she had a very strong sense of fair play. It was the fact that she regarded both men as rogues and her conviction that the pendulum could so easily have swung either way—with regard to who ended up with all the wealth—that governed her bequests to you.' He gave another of those surprisingly warm chuckles. 'Her actual words were that, had Joe Marley and Robert Blake not been such hot-headed fools, you and her grandson would have been co-inheritors. By the terms of her will, she hoped to redress the balance.'

'I suppose I should feel gratitude,' sighed Jane, still

peculiarly numbed. 'But I'm just an ordinary person. . . I simply wouldn't know what to do with so much wealth.'

'Power, rather than wealth,' murmured Marcus Watson. 'It's true that on paper your half of Blake Enterprises is worth a considerable fortune. But, by the terms of the company's charter, the only person to whom you could sell your share is Daniel Blake and, wealthy though that young man undoubtedly is, I doubt if even he could come up with the sort of money necessary to buy you out. And, according to the terms of Mrs Blake's will, the same goes for the house—the grandson is the only person to whom you may sell your share and there are no circumstances under which either could coerce the other into buying or selling.'

'This might sound inordinately ungrateful,' mused Jane, 'but there seem to be rather a lot of strings attached to the late Mrs Blake's generosity.'

'No more than she felt would have been attached had your grandfather and her husband remained in partnership,' pointed out the solicitor, then added, 'Something that puzzled my late client and, I have to confess, I now also find a little puzzling is what prompted you to take up employment with the company with which your family has had such painful association.'

Jane hesitated, colour suddenly warming her cheeks. The secretarial agency with which she had registered on leaving college four years previously had lined up three interviews with prospective employers for her. She had found it more than a little ironic that the second should be with Blake Enterprises and had intended rejecting it out of hand. . .but she had been unable to resist the demon that had materialised within her and urged her to attend the interview. She had done so with a picture in her mind of the brilliance she would display, which would result in the entire board of directors of the company begging her on bended knee to join them.

'I needed a job,' she muttered awkwardly. 'And Blake Enterprises just happened to be offering what I was looking for.'

Needless to say, there had been no board of directors grovelling before her in stunned admiration. She had been interviewed by a spontaneously friendly woman in her mid-twenties whose cheerfully frank enthusiasm for the company in which she worked Jane had begun to find most infectious as she'd learned of its innovative policies regarding staff training and promotion within the company—not to mention the well above average rates of pay.

'Both my father and my grandfather were dead by the time I started work,' she expanded slightly, feeling it was required of her. 'And my mother had no objections.'

Marcus Watson nodded in understanding, then glanced down at his watch apologetically.

'I'm afraid I have another client to see shortly,' he announced, rising, then handing her his card. 'If you feel the need to discuss anything with me, once you've had time to digest all this, I shall be only too happy to give whatever help I can.'

Jane rose as he left, her smile of farewell fading slowly as she stood alone with her thoughts in the large, rather sombre room.

She had been offered all three of the jobs for which she had been interviewed, but the opportunities and pay offered by Blake Enterprises had put the other two to shame. As too had the welcoming atmosphere she had sensed at Blake's. Though at nineteen she had been somewhat impressionable, she remembered wryly. She had taken unreservedly to the friendly personnel officer who had interviewed her;

and she had been just as unreservedly bowled over by the startling good looks of the tall, impeccably suited man who had dashed into the lift behind her after her interview and who had flirted with her with a sophisticated ease that had left her breathless as she'd helped him retrieve the papers that had slipped from the file in his hand while he had propelled his lean athlete's body between the closing doors of the lift.

Extremely impressionable, she informed herself disparagingly, glancing at her watch and deciding she had better call in at her own office before seeing Daniel Blake.

She paused by her assistant's desk—the desk that had been hers until six months ago, when Beth Anderson, the person who had originally interviewed her, had left to get married in Australia.

She smiled, waiting patiently as Lyn Burton shook her head in mute warning and doggedly continued her work at the word processor.

'Sorry about that,' grinned Lyn as she finished. 'But you know tact isn't my strongest point—and that was a letter calling for the utmost tact.'

'You haven't tackled the letter of warning to Joan Sellers, have you?' asked Jane, pulling a small face. 'Lyn, you're an absolute treasure!' she exclaimed when Lyn nodded proudly. 'That was one thing I intended dealing with today, even if it were the only thing!'

'I had the time, and you were otherwise occupied with mysterious solicitors,' replied Lyn, plainly dying to hear what had happened.

'I'll tell you over lunch—I promise,' sighed Jane, hastily pushing the bewildering past couple of hours to the back of her mind. 'I honestly haven't the time now—I just popped back to see if there were any messages.'

'Only a few—they're on your desk,' replied Lyn. 'One of them's from your brother-in-law's estate agent—he wants you to ring him. And Danny Boy rang twice—he wants to see you, you lucky devil!'

'Lyn, one of these days he's going to hear what you've christened him,' chuckled Jane as she opened the door of her own spacious office.

'Who cares, if it makes that perfect specimen of manhood sit up and notice me for once?' sighed Lyn theatrically.

Jane walked to her desk and began scanning through her messages, smiling as the strains of 'O Danny Boy' wafted through the open door.

The truth was that she was sick with apprehension at the prospect of having to face 'Danny Boy', she admitted ruefully to herself. . .a feeling she knew to be totally irrational but one over which she had no control.

She had been with the company for well over six months, and been loving every minute of it, when she'd discovered that the Adonis she had encountered in the lift was none other than Daniel Blake— the young man left with the daunting task of running a multi-million pound organisation on the deaths, a year previously, of both his father and grandfather in a plane crash.

It had been more than a year after Jane's joining the company that Daniel Blake had come across her alone in the duplicating-room just before Christmas. He had kissed her under the mistletoe she hadn't even noticed hanging above her head; and no man who had come into her life since had ever been able to resurrect in her the breathless, tingling excitement she had experienced for those few brief moments in Daniel Blake's arms.

Which only went to show her attitude to men was almost as juvenile as Lyn's, she told herself angrily, picking up the phone and dialling the estate agent's number. Except that Lyn had her tongue firmly in her cheek while she swooned, she reminded herself sharply.

There was a preoccupied look on her face when, a couple of minutes later, she closed the door of her office behind her.

'That's all I needed!' she exclaimed in answer to Lyn's enquiring look. 'You remember I told you those people who'd bought Jenny's and Peter's flat had said they wouldn't be moving in for a couple of months? Well, the estate agent now tells me they've changed their plans and want to move in the day after tomorrow!'

With Lyn's sympathetic response in her ears, she made her way down carpeted corridors to the lift. But, by the time she had reached the top-floor executive suite, her irritation with her accommodation woes had been supplanted by a now almost sickening sensation of apprehension. And the feeling *was* totally irrational, she remonstrated with herself as she swung through the doors leading to the reception area.

'If you're looking for Jacky, she's had to pop out,' the receptionist greeted her.

'No, it's Mr Blake I want to see—he's expecting me,' called out Jane as she strode on and into the absent secretary's office.

Her stride faltered slightly as she approached the open door of Daniel Blake's office. But it was the angry sound of his voice that brought her to a halt.

'I don't believe this! You're telling me that some little jumped-up typist now has as much say as I have in the running of this company?'

'Technically—yes,' replied a voice Jane didn't recognise. 'Though I'm sure it's highly unlikely she would even consider exercising that right. And as for her being a jumped-up little typist, I understood her to be the company's personnel officer.'

'Damn it, James, why split hairs?' exploded Daniel Blake angrily. 'All the Marley woman was, when she ferreted her way in here a few years ago, was a typist! Goodness only knows what her intentions were, but the mere fact that she used an alias speaks volumes. And now I'm to be expected to share my house with the bloody woman!'

Pale, and shaking with a rage like none she had ever experienced before, Jane turned on her heel and re-entered the receptionist's office.

'Judy, Mr Blake appears to have someone with him,' she stated, making a superhuman effort to retain control over herself. 'Would you mind giving him a buzz and asking if he still wishes to see me?'

She had had no intention whatever of interfering with the running of the company, she told herself angrily, taking several deep breaths in an effort to steady herself as the receptionist carried out her request. In fact, she now realised that there had been an equally irrational element of guilt in her feelings of apprehension towards him. . . Without con- sciously thinking about it, her intention had actually been to tell him she would forgo her rights to a share in what she knew had always been his family home!

'Mr Blake says it's all right for you to go in.'

She thanked Judy, squared her shoulders and then retraced her steps towards Daniel Blake's office. Whatever her previous intentions had been, they had now altered—though to what exactly, the terrible rage simmering unabated within her made imposs- ible to define.

It was a sandy-haired, stockily built man who approached her as she entered the office.

'Miss Ashford,' he greeted her, stretching out his hand. 'I'm James Taylor, a friend of Dan's——'

'The woman's name is Marley,' came Daniel Blake's growled interruption from where he lounged, blackly scowling, at his desk. 'And you're here because you also happen to be my solicitor.'

'My name has been Ashford since I was four,' stated Jane, ignoring the interruption as she returned the man's handshake. 'My stepfather adopted me when he and my mother married.'

'Oh, I see!' exclaimed James Taylor, glancing encouragingly towards the man now displaying no interest whatever in the proceedings.

Obviously embarrassed by his friend-cum-client's boorish attitude, the solicitor began fussing around Jane, drawing out a chair and almost pleading with her to be seated.

'Naturally Dan needed me to check the small print—so to speak—in his grandmother's will, and——'

'Let's cut the pussyfooting, shall we?' snapped Daniel Blake, coming to sudden life as he straightened in his swivel chair and fixed Jane with the implacable animosity of his gaze. 'To put things in a nutshell, buying out your share in the company is financially out of the question, much to my regret,' he informed her harshly. 'So I've decided you shall receive the same percentage of the company's profits as I do and my grandmother did. You will, of course, resign your position here—and anyway, your present salary is peanuts compared to the dividend you'll be receiving.'

Beside her Jane heard James Taylor's stifled groan of exasperation.

'I'll have the house valued,' continued Daniel Blake, 'and I'll buy out your half at fifty per cent of the highest price quoted.' That said, he leaned his large frame back in the chair, his scowling expression switching to one of bored indifference.

'And now that you've had your say, perhaps you'd like to hear what I've decided,' stated Jane with a quiet calm completely at variance with the rage of fury boiling within her. 'I shall *not* be resigning my position here, but I *shall* be taking my rightful seat on the board of directors.' She rose, just as Daniel Blake straightened once more in his chair, his face now a picture of fury and disbelief. 'And as for my share in the house—I shan't be selling it.' She made her way unhurriedly to the door. 'In fact, I shall be moving my things in the day after tomorrow.'

'Oh, boy, what I wouldn't give to have been a fly on the wall!' exclaimed Lyn, glancing down at the lunch that had remained untouched before her as she had drunk in Jane's every word. 'A jumped-up typist, indeed!'

'Don't tell me I detect a note of criticism in your tone—directed at your precious Danny Boy,' murmured Jane, feeling suddenly totally drained.

'I've always been one to place friendship before lust,' retorted Lyn, grinning. 'And, besides, I know which side my bread's buttered. You know, I think I'll send out a memo—in triplicate—to Joan Sellers, stating that forelocks are to be respectfully tugged in the presence of our new——'

'Lyn, for heaven's sake!' groaned Jane, horrified. 'I don't want one word of *any* of this getting out!'

A slightly startled look replaced Lyn's grin. 'Jane. . .heck, you *know* that if any of this does get out, not a single syllable of it will have come from me!'

'Of course I know that,' sighed Jane apologetically. 'It's just that. . .Lyn, I'm still so befuddled by all that's happened, my sense of humour seems to have deserted me.'

'I've a feeling mine would have too,' sympathised

Lyn, then suddenly ran her fingers through her cropped, shining auburn hair in a gesture of perplexity. 'Heck, every sense I possess would probably have deserted me had I just learned out of the blue that I'd become a millionairess!'

'On paper,' Jane reminded her, the words sounding almost dazed. 'I've a feeling that even if I pinched myself non-stop every other second for the next couple of hours, I still wouldn't completely believe all this.'

Lyn laughed as she began tucking into her food. 'Don't worry, you'll be able to believe it soon enough,' she chuckled. 'And one thing guaranteed to restore your sense of humour is the thought of the look on Danny Boy's face when you move in on Saturday—I'll be only too happy to give you a hand with the move.'

Jane, who had just taken a mouthful of food, swallowed it so hastily she almost choked.

'Lyn, I only *said* that!' she squeaked in protest. 'I've no intention whatsoever of actually moving into the place.'

'What on earth do you mean?' demanded Lyn. 'For heaven's sake, Jane—you're homeless as of Saturday and you've just been handed half a virtual palace on a platter.' She broke off, eyeing Jane with disbelief. 'Jane, you have seen this place the delectable Danny Boy inhabits, haven't you?'

Jane shook her head, laughing as Lyn rolled her eyes theatrically.

'It's colossal—all virginal white and terribly elegant. And it must have at least a dozen—well, I'm sure a good six—bedrooms.' She grinned wickedly across the table. 'If it's worry about not being able to keep your hands off all that manly perfection that's holding you back, forget it—you could go forever without bumping into one another in a place that size.'

Jane was conscious of the colour having risen in her cheeks, though she wasn't certain whether its cause was Lyn's joking reference to her not being able to keep her hands off Daniel Blake, or those humiliatingly dismissive references of his to her as 'jumped-up typist' and 'that bloody woman' now echoing tautingly in her head.

'Jane, let's face it—the chances of your finding anywhere between now and Saturday are nil,' pointed out Lyn. 'And it would be an act of madness, anyway, even to consider looking.'

'Lyn, I can see the sense in what you're saying,' admitted Jane reluctantly, 'but things are bad enough with him as it is. . .it would only create even more unpleasantness.'

'You mean *he* would only create more unpleasantness,' stated Lyn quietly. 'When Joan Sellers started creating unpleasantness in her department, you were the one who stood up to her. . .you're the one who's found jobs in other departments for the two people who would have resigned rather than work another minute with her, and you're the one who's told her that if another member of her staff decides to leave because of her, you're going to have to refer the matter to Danny Boy with a view to having her fired.'

'I said that?' gasped Jane.

'Don't worry—I worded it excruciatingly tactfully,' murmured Lyn. 'And that was what I gathered you intended saying—or did I misunderstand you?'

Jane shook her head, then gave a sigh of exasperation. 'Anyway, there's no comparison,' she protested half-heartedly. 'All right, I can make moves towards getting Joan fired if she doesn't mend her ways—but who's going to evict Danny Boy if he doesn't mend his?'

'Ah, but the chances are he will,' murmured Lyn dreamily. 'And who knows? The two of you might live happily ever after.'

'And you, my dozy friend, are wasted in personnel,' groaned Jane weakly. 'You should be writing science fiction.'

CHAPTER TWO

THE house, Jane found, actually managed to live up to a substantial proportion of Lyn's extravagant claims on its behalf. It stood elegant and aloof behind high red-brick walls and heavy wrought-iron gates, conveying a confident appearance of being situated in the spaciousness of meadowed countryside instead of in one of land-starved London's more exclusive areas.

With her heart beating in a heavy rhythm of dread, and wishing she had given in to Lyn's pleas to accompany her, Jane got out of the battered van she had hired, in which lay the sum total of her worldly possessions, and tried the huge gates.

It was obviously asking too much to have expected Daniel to have opened them for her, she thought resignedly as she heaved apart both sections. Though, from his drowsily monosyllabic responses to her phone call an hour earlier, it wouldn't surprise her to learn he had gone back to the sleep from which her call had so obviously dragged him. She glanced down at her watch as she got back into the van—it was gone eleven, for heaven's sake!

She muttered exasperatedly to herself as she found the van's access to the front door of the house blocked by a navy BMW sports car and another red car. Though she was unable to put a name to the make of the second car, it looked every bit as smugly expensive as the other.

She yanked on the handbrake and switched off the engine, cursing audibly. Convinced that both cars had been positioned with the express purpose of hampering her access, she leapt from the van and raced up the three steps to the house. She located a large brass doorbell, placed her finger on its button and kept it there.

'For heaven's sake, must you?' demanded the tall, elegantly dishevelled vision who finally opened the door.

The vision would have been stunningly beautiful had she not looked so bad-tempered, thought Jane, the complete unexpectedness of the woman's appearance leaving her momentarily dumb-struck.

'Well? What do you want?' demanded the apparition with a total lack of grace, just as Jane had startled and slightly shocked herself with the assumption that she was face to face with the cause of Daniel Blake's reluctance to leave his bed.

'I don't *want* anything,' Jane informed her with a haughtiness hitherto unknown to her. 'I live here.'

The woman took an involuntary step back, her sullen expression altering to one of open incredulity.

'Daniel!' she yelled, without turning her gaze from Jane and with a volume that was ear-shattering. 'There's a girl on your doorstep claiming she lives here.'

Jane had begun seriously contemplating pinching herself in an effort to gauge if this could possibly be real, when the woman gave a sudden shriek of terror as a huge golden retriever pushed its way past her and came to a halt before Jane.

'You've let that wretched dog out again!' shrieked the woman, again making full use of her surprisingly powerful lungs.

'For heaven's sake, Amanda, stop screeching like that,' came Daniel Blake's disembodied yell of a reply.

The dog sat down and gazed up at Jane from heart-breakingly gentle brown eyes.

'You're mad!' exclaimed the woman, leaping back as Jane reached out a hand to stroke the dog. 'He's likely to take your hand off!'

Jane immediately withdrew her hand, which the dog promptly stretched towards and licked.

'Here, Flynn!'

The retriever responded instantly to his master's call as Daniel Blake appeared in the doorway, belting around him the bathrobe he had obviously just donned for the sake of decency.

'Would somebody mind removing those cars?' demanded Jane, the urge to pinch herself increasing with every passing second. 'They're blocking my——'

'Daniel, who *is* this woman?' demanded Amanda aggressively.

'Second shift reporting for duty,' drawled Daniel, his cold eyes sweeping over Jane's denim-clad figure as his hand reached out to stroke the dog at his side. 'So you'd better run along before things start hotting up, Amanda. And besides, Flynn hasn't had his breakfast yet and I'm not sure I have the strength to restrain him.'

The dog's ears pricked up at the sound of his name, then he flopped down at his master's feet with a noisy sigh.

For several seconds there was silence while Amanda looked suspiciously from the dog to his master.

'I don't find this in the least amusing,' she snapped eventually, manging to include Jane in the disgruntled look she gave both man and dog. 'But I might have guessed someone like you would, Daniel.' She took keys from her bag and swept past Jane down the steps to the red car.

'I hope you don't have a similar effect on all my female visitors,' drawled Daniel, hugging his arms to his chest as he leaned a shoulder against the door. 'Otherwise my sex-life's going to be in a very sorry state.'

'Would you mind removing the other car?' demanded Jane through clenched teeth. 'I still can't get near enough to the house.'

His expression one of bland indifference, he gazed past her, frowning suddenly as he caught sight of the van.

'I hope you haven't any ideas about moving a load of tat in here—I like my surroundings just the way they are.'

'Just move the car, will you?' hissed Jane, the little that was left of her patience fast disappearing.

'Don't you think you should come in and have a look around before you start bringing your things in?' he enquired. 'After all, you could easily hate the place.'

The slight tinge of evil in the grin with which he responded to Jane's shrug of acquiescence made her hesitate.

'You haven't by any chance a bucket of water balanced over the door and waiting to drown me the moment I enter, have you?' she asked, joking in a desperate attempt to distract her body from its over-powering urge to turn and flee.

'You'd best come in and find out for yourself,' he replied, his laughter soft and rumbling as he turned back inside, the dog rising and following him.

'Did you live here with your grandmother?' she asked, still needing distraction from her urge to run even as she stepped through the doorway and into a huge, parquet-floored hall.

'No—she and my grandfather tended to spend most of their time in the West Indies after he retired. And she more often than not preferred staying in an hotel whenever she visited England. . .she claimed I was too exhausting to live with.'

He halted as he reached the wide sweep of the magnificent staircase dominating the hall, chuckling softly to himself in a way that sent a shiver of apprehension through Jane.

Refusing to be intimidated, she glanced upwards and found herself looking up at the clear blue of the sky through a large circular window set in the roof and surrounded by a series of smaller skylights.

Daniel turned, hooking an arm over the carved banister beside him as he faced her.

'Well, I suppose that, now you're actually here, we might as well discuss how we're going to divide up the place,' he drawled, something close to anger gleaming in the chill depths of his eyes as they drilled into hers. 'What do you propose—stringing up sheets across the centre of each room?'

'Oh, for heaven's sake!' burst out Jane in exasperation. 'Surely we can agree on something more civilised than that, Mr——' She bit back the words, furious with herself for the fact she had been about to address him as 'Mr Blake', which she knew would have sounded quite ludicrous.

'You were saying, Miss Marley?' he taunted.

'The name's Ashford—as you well know,' retorted Jane stiffly, pride and that alone keeping her from turning on her heel and running. 'But quite frankly I'd rather you just called me Jane.'

'And I certainly shall,' he murmured. 'After all, it would be a little odd if two people as intimately acquainted as we are weren't on first name terms. By the way, I do hope you'll remind me to get in plenty of mistletoe for Christmas.' He broke off, his expression feigning surprise while his knowing eyes leisurely took in the splashes of scarlet now staining her cheeks. 'You *do* remember our titillating encounter under the mistletoe, don't you, Jane. . .how many years ago was it now?'

'Too many for me to remember,' snapped Jane, and wished she hadn't when she felt her cheeks burn an even deeper shade of scarlet.

'How disappointing,' he murmured silkily. 'And to think I always deluded myself that our romantic Christmas encounter had had the same profound effect on you as it had on me; led on, no doubt, by those lingering glances we've tended to exchange ever since on those infrequent occasions we meet.'

The temptation to cut her losses and run was one Jane would now have found irresistible had not her legs become immovable lead weights.

'Strange, isn't it, that you should have been the one woman ever to cause me to reconsider my self-imposed rule about not fraternising with my female staff?'

It was as he was uttering those last words—words that filled her with a feeling so peculiar she refused even to attempt to define it—that the dog came padding towards them, carrying a large plastic bowl in his mouth. Jane could almost have flung her arms around him in gratitude for the distraction he provided as he placed his bowl at his master's feet and gazed soulfully up at him.

'Poor old fellow, you still haven't had your porridge, have you?' asked Daniel softly, reaching down and scratching the dog's ears affectionately.

He picked up the bowl, glancing at Jane as he straightened. 'There's a spare set of keys in the dashboard of my car—perhaps you'd care to move it while I see to Flynn?'

The day was drawing towards evening by the time Jane returned to her new home, having delivered back the hired van. But the leaden feeling of apprehension she had been experiencing on and off ever since hearing the terms of Dolly Blake's will had now taken on a depressing permanency.

It wasn't going to work, she told herself as she walked down a tree-lined avenue, the din of the traffic-filled street she had just turned off growing fainter with each step she took.

From the blue, a picture of her grandfather sprang to her mind. Her mother always said there was quite a bit of him in her—mostly the good, but a liberal sprinkling of the bad too. She had his fiery temper, she admitted, and also a good measure of his pig-headed stubbornness. Her steps faltered slightly as she also admitted that it was that pig-headed stubbornness that would force her to see this through. . .despite her knowing that it would never work. And the main reason, no, the *only* reason, because she had the mental stamina to see most things through—was that she was locked in this crazy, surreal battle with a man to whom she had felt overpoweringly attracted the first moment she had set eyes on him and towards whom she still felt every bit as strongly attracted.

She felt her cheeks burn once more as she remembered his disconcertingly taunting remark about her having been the one woman to make him reconsider his self-imposed rules regarding fraternising with his female staff. . .and that was all he had been doing, she told herself impatiently—taunting her with whatever weapon happened to come to hand. Admittedly he had helped her carry in her things, but only because good manners had demanded it of him; that he had made abundantly clear.

But he had left her alone to choose which of the remaining five bedrooms she wanted—doing no more than indicating the sixth and informing her it was his. Though there was little in it, she had decided on a large, elegantly understated room with its *en suite* bathroom and lavish amount of cupboard space. She had chosen it for its magnificent view, overlooking the shrub-edged lawn at the back of the house.

She had felt like objecting, but uncharacteristically hadn't, when he had later opened the door of her room and strolled in uninvited.

'So this is the one you've decided on,' he had observed coolly, and then strode out.

It had crossed her mind to lock the door, but Flynn, who had accompanied him in, had decided to stay and investigate the alien jumble disturbing the once ordered serenity of the room. . .and it would have gone against her nature, anyway, to have taken so outlandish a step as locking the door.

She halted as she reached the house, surprised to find the gates she had so painstakingly closed behind her now wide open. Her heart sank as she noticed too that the car was gone.

She ascended the steps and rang the bell. This was all she needed, she thought frustratedly—he could be gone all night for all she knew, and it hadn't even occurred to her to ask him for a key. He should have offered her one, she told herself angrily—especially if he'd intended going out.

Anger boiling inside her, she sat down on the steps. He had planned it all and she had fallen right into his trap!

Damn all Blakes! she raged. Yet, as the years had passed, she had tended towards her mother's pragmatic view of the feud—that there was no sense living in the past, especially one so painful. But this was the present, and Daniel Blake showed every sign of being able to teach his scheming and treacherous grandfather a trick or two. Well, she wasn't Joe Marley's granddaughter for nothing; she would

teach—— Her turgidly bloodthirsty train of thought
came to an abrupt halt as the BMW swept through
the gates and screeched to a halt by the steps. She
remained seated, struggling to keep her face
expressionless as she contended with the series of
somersaults her stomach launched into when Daniel
Blake stepped out of the car.

'Out you come, old fellow,' he called to Flynn,
completely ignoring Jane's presence.

Jane rose, feeling much as she felt a beggar would
feel asking for alms. . . She *owned* half the place,
damn it!

'How old is Flynn?' she asked, startling herself
slightly.

He closed the car door. 'Eighteen months—why?'

'It's just that you referred to him as old,' she called
out, wishing she hadn't started the conversation as
he walked to the gates and closed them.

She bent down and hugged the dog who had come
bounding up to her as though delighted to see her.

'It's a term of endearment,' he informed her when
he eventually reached her side, glancing down at her
with her arms still round Flynn with a faintly disapproving look. 'I suppose I'll have to give you a key,'
he added ungraciously, inserting his own into the
lock.

'There isn't any suppose about it,' snapped Jane,
sweeping in past him with her nose in the air and
promptly stumbling over Flynn.

Daniel caught her by the arm to steady her, then
turned her to face him.

'They say pride comes before a fall,' he reminded
her with icy softness. 'And I wouldn't advise your
ever using that tone of voice with me again.'

'I'll use whatever tone I wish,' she retorted heat-
edly, furious with herself for the heart-pounding

response of her body to his sudden nearness. 'And if you think——'

His mouth silenced hers in the bruising sudden-ness of a kiss that stunned her to inaction. It was a kiss that was initially almost cold in its calculating deliberation, but which swiftly warmed to a sensual softness as his arms encircled her, drawing her body against the muscled leanness of his while her own arms rose involuntarily to wind around his neck. There were too many intoxicating sensations bombarding her for there to be any room in her mind for thought, and it was her body that took over, melting to the commands of the sure hands that moulded it to the tensing heat of his, while her lips gave nothing but encouragement in their wild response to the increasing demands being imposed on them.

'Your half or mine?' he whispered, suddenly removing his mouth from hers and starting to bite against her lower lip with a sharp insistence she found mind-blowingly erotic.

'What?' croaked Jane, freezing for an instant then tearing herself from his arms as the utterly alien intensity of her reaction jolted her into an automatic rejection of it.

'I was wondering whose half of the house we should make love in,' he said, gazing down at her from eyes that were narrowed slits, and making no attempt to take her back in his arms. 'Though, as we've only decided on two of the six bedrooms——'

'Would you mind showing me the kitchen?' demanded Jane, a self-preserving instinct compelling her to ignore what had just happened even though her mind gave out dire warnings as to the likely consequences of so ludicrous a ploy.

'You want us to make love in the kitchen?' he asked, parodying wide-eyed innocence. 'Personally, I think we should opt for a bed the first time——'

'I'd like a cup of tea—I'm thirsty.' She realised she probably sounded like an unmitigated idiot, but she didn't care—there was no way she intended acknowledging what had happened. 'And I really do think we ought to talk.'

'Whereas I'd rather get on with the action,' he drawled. 'But I suppose you have a point—we might as well get the talking over and done with.' He began moving off down the hall, Flynn at his heels. 'Come on—we'll introduce you to the kitchen.'

He left her at the doorway, sauntering across a floor tiled in rich hues of burnt umber, which had undoubtedly cost a small fortune, and picked up a kettle which he filled at a large double sink. The floor was magnificent, thought Jane, still rooted to the spot where he had left her. But could the rest of it really be described as a kitchen?

At the far end of the room were huge Georgian veranda doors and before them a vertitable jungle of pot plants, most of which had the appearance of being in the last throes of neglect. There was a large scrubbed-wood table with several chairs around it, which effectively blocked the path from the sink to a large, cumbersome-looking cooker which stood in isolation as though it had been dumped there and no one had got around to positioning it anywhere else. Apart from a large Welsh dresser, in the same scrubbed-wood as the table, and a free-standing fridge-freezer, there was nothing else in the room to strengthen its claim to being a kitchen.

'It usually has that effect—on women, anyway,' stated Daniel, plugging in the kettle on the draining-board of one of the sinks, then leaning back with his arms folded as he waited for it to boil.

'It's. . .well, it's not exactly what you'd call functional, is it?' muttered Jane, walking to the table and drawing out a chair.

Daniel shrugged, glancing round him with a surprisingly uncritical eye. 'It's certainly not the way it was supposed to be. . .perhaps the next time I get involved with an interior designer I'll wait till she's finished messing about with the house before I end the relationship.'

Jane was unable to hide her amusement, for which she received a glacial look.

'Why didn't you get someone in to finish it off?' she asked, as he went to the dresser and began preparing a tray.

'I never got around to it,' he replied, placing the tray on the table and then returning to the sink to make the tea. 'Perhaps you'd like to take on the task?'

Jane gazed around her, pulling a face—it was a nightmare as it was.

'I suppose I could make some enquiries about getting something done. . .anything would be preferable to this,' she added candidly. 'How long has it been in this state?'

'I can't remember—less than a year,' he replied, going to the fridge and returning to the table with a milk jug. 'I hope you don't take sugar, because I don't think there is any,' he announced, sitting down and shoving the tray across the table towards Jane. 'You can pour.'

Jane was gazing at him in disbelief. 'How on earth have you managed all this time? There are practically no work-surfaces!'

He gave her a rather guarded look as she began pouring the tea.

'Nettie, my ex-housekeeper, was a bit peeved to start with, but she seemed to manage all right. . .mind you, she did leave because she said she'd had enough of the place.'

Jane took a hasty sip from her cup to stop herself

bursting out laughing—he had sounded genuinely surprised by his housekeeper's desertion!

'The other two housekeepers I've had since weren't exactly ecstatic over it either—the second finished working off a week's notice only yesterday.' He picked up his cup and took a drink from it, his eyes narrowing speculatively over the rim as he gazed across the table at her. 'Can you cook?' he demanded suddenly.

'Yes,' she replied warily. 'But, even if this were a dream-kitchen, I've no intention of stepping into your housekeeper's shoes just because I'm living here. And I'm sure, had I been a man, the thought wouldn't even have crossed your mind,' she added sharply.

'You can get off your liberated high horse,' he retorted, just as sharply, 'because I'm not fussy what sex the person doing the cooking is.'

'Are you telling me you're not capable of cooking yourself a meal?'

'I'd hardly be asking you to do it for me if I were,' he snapped. 'And you're not being asked to step into the role of housekeeper. Nettie fixed me up with someone who comes in for a few hours each weekday to clean up the place and do the washing and ironing. . . I suppose she realised I'd not have much luck replacing her. I did offer to send the cleaning woman on a cookery course,' he muttered, picking up his cup once more. 'I got the impression she thought I was joking.'

Jane gazed down at the table, a heated discussion taking place in her head.

'All right, I'll do the cooking,' she said quietly—at least the fact that he had asked her might be regarded as a measure of his acceptance of her presence. 'But you'll have to do the shopping—it's only fair you do your share.'

The look he gave her was enough to kill, but it was followed by an almost imperceptible shrug of acquiescence.

'I'd be grateful if you'd get cracking on the kitchen, though,' he said, a gleam of mockery in the blue eyes meeting hers. 'Because then I shan't have quite so much trouble finding a housekeeper once you've left.'

Jane gave a sudden start as she felt something nudge against her leg, then relaxed as she realised it was Flynn. She reached down and stroked him, returning Daniel's mocking look with one of open challenge.

'You might as well accept it, Daniel Blake—I shan't be leaving.'

'I think it's you who should be accepting how heavily the odds are stacked against you, Jane Marley.' There was a chilling undertone in the quietness of his words. 'There are innumerable ways I could make life so unpleasant for you here that your only option would be to leave eventually. . .but it's not really necessary for me to resort to unpleasantness, is it?' He leaned back in his chair, a lazy insolence in the eyes that swept over her, lingering a while on the soft fullness of a mouth still unnaturally reddened by its passionate encounter with his, before moving down to the well-defined curve of her breasts beneath the pale denim of her shirt. 'I've already admitted to having been tempted by the idea of an affair with you. . .but, with the two of us now under the same roof, the realisation of that idea seems pretty much an inevitability, wouldn't you agree?'

The word 'yes' leapt unchecked into Jane's mind, the unequivocal certainty with which every part of her so spontaneously accepted a concept she hadn't even considered, let alone examined, shocking her profoundly.

'I'm sorry, but I'm having difficulty finding any logic in your rather amazing statement,' she replied, flabbergasted by the calmness of her own unrushed words. 'Looking at it purely hypothetically, I'd have thought the best place to have a woman with whom you intended having an affair would be under your roof. . .it seems to me it would save you quite a bit of inconvenience.'

'Why bring hypothesis into it?' he murmured. 'Surely you don't deny the strong, and decidedly mutual, sexual attraction between us?'

'I'm afraid we're talking at cross purposes,' exclaimed Jane, the calmness that had so astounded her now all but deserting her. '*You* might regard a vague feeling of sexual attraction as sufficient reason to launch into an affair—*I* most certainly don't!'

'I can promise you, there's nothing in the least vague in the nature of my feelings towards you,' he informed her with an assurance she found both infuriating and enviable. 'And I really shouldn't have to point out that, despite those feelings, I resisted the idea of an affair with you. . .until fate, in the guise of my misguided grandmother, stepped in.'

'Your grandmother seems to have been the only member of the Blake family with any sense of honour——'

'Something the Marleys possess in abundance?' he drawled. 'The business world doesn't set much store by airy-fairy talk about honour, shocking though it may seem to people like you and my grandmother. With the sudden deaths of my father and grand-father, the company's turnover suffered as a result of the business market's uncertainty over whether a man as a young as I was had what it took to take over sole control of a concern as diversified as Blake Enterprises.' He picked up his cup and took a leisurely sip from it. 'Fortunately I proved my worth in a relatively short time. But the repercussions of its getting out that the company was being co-run by some bird-brain hell-bent on avenging a grandfather with more temper than sense——'

'How dare you——?'

'Would have a catastrophic effect on the company's performance,' he continued ruthlessly. 'There's nothing I can do to change my grandmother's ludicrous will—but there's a hell of a lot I can to do minimise its effect. Getting you out of my house won't present too many problems and neither, I hope, will getting you out of my business——'

'*Your* house—*your* business?' cut in Jane, shaking with anger. 'I own fifty per cent of both, and you'll get me out of neither!'

'Oh no?' he murmured softly, his eyes glittering chips of ice as they held hers. 'As I've already pointed out, it's inevitable that we shall have an affair. . .the strong sexual attraction between us is something I intend exploiting to the full. It's when that affair has run its course that you will move out of my house. . .and you'll do so simply because your pride won't let you remain once I've lost interest in you. Though how long that will take—my losing interest, that is—we have yet to find out.'

CHAPTER THREE

'THERE was a meeting of the directors yesterday—why wasn't I informed?' demanded Jane, closing the door of Daniel's office behind her and marching across to his desk.

'I wasn't aware of having an appointment with you this morning,' stated Daniel, glancing up briefly from the papers strewn across the desk-top.

'Don't you think it's about time you dispensed with this pettiness?' asked Jane wearily. 'You refuse to discuss business at home, yet I've been trying to make an appointment to see you here for the past four days—and with no success.'

'Perhaps I've been too busy shopping to have any spare time——'

'And perhaps not!' countered Jane angrily. 'It's common knowledge that you've been sending your clerical staff out to do it.'

'OK—so, now you've caught me alone, you might as well get what you have to say off your chest.' He glanced down at the wafer-thin gold of the watch nestling against the dark hairs at his wrist. 'I should be able to spare you a couple of minutes.'

'How gracious of you,' observed Jane acidly, pointedly taking the seat he had failed to offer her. 'We'll start with the meeting——'

'Which I called in order to explain the implications of my grandmother's will. There was absolutely no reason for you to be present. But if you insist on attending future board meetings——'

'Which I do.'

'Then I shall see you're provided with the relevant

paperwork. But I think I should point out to you that the board of directors of Blake Enterprises—apart from me—is completely non-executive.' The cold challenge in his eyes as he spoke filled her with hopeless exasperation.

'And the last thing you want is a vindictive avenger like me meddling—is that it?' she sighed. 'You may find this hard to believe, but I have nothing but admiration for the administrative policies of the company, and all I want is to become familiar with how the actual operating part of it functions. . .after all, your grandmother has given me that right and I don't consider I'm asking the impossible.'

'Don't you?' he enquired drily. 'It's because this organisation is so diverse and complex that we need consultant directors of the calibre of ours—each man is an expert in his own field. My job is to weigh up the advice of those experts—whether it be concerning the structural engineering side of the company or any of half a dozen other areas in which we operate— and act accordingly. It's a job I do well because it's one I was rigorously groomed for by my father and grandfather.' He gave his watch an impatient glance. 'Was there anything else you wanted to discuss?' he demanded abruptly.

Jane nodded. 'You haven't replied to my memo regarding Joan Sellers.'

'No, I haven't,' he replied. 'But now is as good a time as any to inform you that your job here is to engage people, not to fire them—not at her level of seniority, anyway.'

'I'm perfectly aware of that,' she replied, determined to mask her reaction to that deliberately demeaning remark, 'which you would be aware of too, had you taken the trouble to read my memo.'

'Not only have I read it, but I've also had a look at Miss Sellers's file. I take it the letter of warning, under your assistant's signature, was sent out under your instruction?' he asked with steely quietness.

'Yes, I. . .' Jane broke off, her heart sinking as she realised she had never got around to reading the letter Lyn had composed. She took a deep breath, then continued. 'Though staff problems are a fortunate rarity here, Beth Anderson—my predecessor—made a point of briefing me on the relevant procedure. She did so mainly because she had already had the need to give Miss Sellers a verbal warning.'

'How's Beth finding Australia?' he asked out of the blue.

'Fine. . .she. . .she loves it,' managed Jane, annoyed to find herself so thrown by the unexpectedness of his question that she was reduced to stammering.

'I hear your mother and stepfather live there. He's in medicine, isn't he?'

She nodded, hardly believing her ears and wondering from where he could possibly have obtained this information.

'And hasn't your stepsister and her husband—a doctor, too, I believe—recently joined them there from London?'

Jane gazed across the desk at him, suspicion in her eyes—it was as though he had decided to spell out to her the ease with which he could delve into her life.

'It seems as though Australia's the in place,' he murmured, his eyes returning her suspicion with open mockery. 'Ever thought of it for yourself? I'm sure you'd love it. . .especially with all your family there.'

For the first time in her twenty-three years, Jane understood what it was to feel goaded almost to the point of violence. She rose to her feet, battling with herself in order not to give vent to the fury of her feelings.

'Knowing how precious your time is, I'll not waste it on idle chit-chat,' she stated woodenly. 'Perhaps you'd be good enough to let me know your intentions regarding Joan Sellers.' She began walking to the door, her back ramrod-straight, then turned only to find him a few steps behind her. 'Preferably before you lose the remainder of the clerical staff from the advertising section.'

'I'll have a think about it,' he said, stepping between Jane and the door. 'I forgot to mention this morning that I shan't be dining in tonight.' A mocking grin hovered on his lips. 'Though, if you'd still like me to do the shopping——'

'That won't be necessary,' snapped Jane, wishing he would move out of her way and let her leave. 'I already told you the kitchen people were starting today. The fact that I shan't be doing any cooking for the next few days will no doubt come as good news to those members of your staff you delegate to do the shopping.'

He chuckled, the sudden intimacy in its softness sending a shiver prickling down her spine. 'Don't worry on their behalf, Jane; they're practically queueing up to do it.' He leaned back against the door, the glittering harshness in his eyes disturbingly at odds with the supple ease of his body. 'They're very much aware that they're shopping for two. . .but I've a feeling it's yet to filter down through the grapevine exactly who that second person is.'

'If you don't mind, I have work to do,' stated Jane, mortified to feel the sting of heat on her cheeks.

'And I mustn't detain you,' he murmured, showing no signs of moving from her path. 'It's strange, though,' he added, his hand reaching out to trace his fingers lightly down the side of her cheek, 'how the prospect of leaving you on your own this evening stirs feelings in me. . .almost of guilt.' His hand dropped to her shoulder. 'Almost as though by seeing another woman I'm guilty of being unfaithful to you.'

'Would you mind letting me out of here?' she asked, her voice noticeably unsteady.

'You sound jittery, Jane,' he whispered. 'You showed no signs of being afraid of me when we had my desk between us,' he taunted, suddenly pulling her sharply against him. 'Yet now your heart is racing. . .what from—fear or excitement?'

Jane felt her body stiffen with a terrible tension as his arms encircled her and his mouth descended on hers to plunder with practised ease. But, as her hands clenched to fists at her sides and her lips clamped to a tight uncooperative line that prevented them from giving in to their every inclination to part and participate in the delights that were theirs for the taking, she knew that his taunting words had been the truth; that the tension within her was her body's only defence against the fierce surge of excitement threatening to overwhelm her.

'If this weren't the wrong time and the wrong place, I'd so easily break through your flimsy defences,' he whispered huskily against her mouth. 'You know that, don't you, Jane?'

'No, I. . .' For an agonising instant her mouth trembled against the coaxing softness of his, then she tore herself away from him with an exclamation of fury. 'Let me go!' she spat, as he caught her by the upper arms, tilting her head back.

'It's only a matter of time, Jane,' he murmured, the calculating coldness of his eyes untouched by the half-smile on his lips. 'Perhaps when I return home tonight it will be to find you in the one part of my house I'd not object to finding you—my bed.'

Her intention to hit him—with a blow behind which she would hurl every ounce of her strength—only reached her consciousness in the moment that he caught her wrist in a vice-like grip that prevented her carrying it out.

'Not a wise move,' he advised her icily, releasing her hand just as swiftly as he had caught it, then reaching over and opening the door.

'Jane!'

The sharp ring of his voice behind her froze her in her frantic dash to freedom.

'If you get a chance, I'd be grateful if you could give Flynn a run in the park this evening.'

'This is fabulous—I've never eaten in a place this posh before!' exclaimed Lyn with enthusiasm, gazing inquisitively around her.

Jane smiled. 'I thought I'd better bring you some-where special to make up for not having had you. . .' she hesitated fractionally before using the word that still didn't come naturally to her even after almost three weeks '. . .home for a meal yet. I'm honestly beginning to believe that wretched kitchen will never be finished.'

'As long as I'm invited to its christening,' grinned Lyn, then tilted her head questioningly to one side. 'That massive bunch of flowers delivered to you today—it wasn't by any chance an apology from Danny Boy, was it?'

Jane shook her head, her expression amused. 'I wondered when you'd get around to asking about that. Actually, they were from Paul French——'

'Your journalist admirer?' exclaimed Lyn. 'But I thought he'd been bundled off somewhere as a foreign correspondent for his paper.'

'He has—but there are such things as holidays,' teased Jane, though only now realising just how little she was looking forward to Paul's return. She liked him, but only as a friend, and Paul had begun persistently demanding a relationship a good deal deeper than friendship just before he had been posted abroad. 'And what exactly is it that you feel Danny Boy should be apologising about?' she enquired.

'Promoting that Sellers woman, for heaven's sake!' exploded Lyn indignantly.

'But at least he's promoted her virtually out of harm's way—and she *is* good at her job, no matter what reservations we may have about her personality,' she added placatingly, then opened her menu and began perusing it.

Lyn threw her a mutinous look, then followed suit, only to return to the subject niggling her so much the instant they had given the waiter their orders.

'Jane, did you actually tell Danny Boy what that woman did?' she demanded, continuing before Jane had any chance to reply. 'And another thing, I bet you were so shocked at the way she went for you over your having reported her to him that it didn't ever occur to you to wonder how it was she found out you had!'

Jane frowned—it hadn't occurred to her. 'Right on both counts,' she admitted wearily. 'But what sort of personnel officer would I be if I were to go running to the managing director every time a member of staff lost her temper with me?'

Lyn gave her a withering look. 'So he promotes her, and now she's crowing like nobody's business,' she observed indignantly, her expression mollifying slightly as waiters appeared with food. 'If I'd been in your shoes,' she continued once the waiters had gone, 'I'd have let her rant on—then I'd have let her know I was now as good as her employer and given her her marching orders!'

'Lyn!' groaned Jane reproachfully.

'I know, I know!' sighed Lyn. 'You don't want people knowing and you don't intend exercising what I, for one, am certain must be your rights. . . You should be nominated for a sainthood!'

Jane gave a wan smile, then gazed down at her plate with little appetite as Lyn tucked in with her customary enthusiasm, her smile suddenly deepening to one of warm affection. Had it not been for her friendship with Lyn—one that had sprung up over three years ago when Lyn had also joined the company—she would have missed her stepsister, Jenny, unbearably. She gazed over at her bubbly, warmhearted friend, acutely conscious that, though there was little that one kept from the other, there was one thing she had always kept from Lyn. . .the powerful attraction she had always felt towards Daniel Blake. Her reticence had nothing to do with Lyn's tongue-in-cheek drooling over Daniel—she had always recognised that for what it was. The truth was it was something she had never been able to confide in anyone—not even to Jenny, from whom she had hidden nothing since they were small children—the effect that Daniel Blake had had on her from the start. And because of that, there was no way she could discuss with Lyn Daniel's calculating wooing of her. . .nor the sometimes almost overpowering strength of the temptation threatening her resolve with each passing day.

'This is delicious,' sighed Lyn, scattering Jane's comfortless thoughts. 'You will be seeing Paul when he comes back, won't you?'

'I thought you didn't like him,' protested Jane, eyeing her quizzically.

'But only because he'd been pressurising you so

heavily before he left,' admitted Lyn. 'But I'm sure by now he's accepted that all you're interested in is his friendship. . .and you could do with getting out and about a bit.'

'You're beginning to sound like my mother,' chuckled Jane, touched, though also faintly alarmed, by the underlying note of anxiety in her friend's words.

'To be honest, there are times when I feel guilty about the way I practically twisted your arm to get you to move in with Danny Boy,' sighed Lyn.

'Lyn, you know me well enough to know that no amount of arm-twisting can force me into something I don't want to do.'

'I know, but. . . Jane, you wouldn't stay put just for the sake of not losing face, would you?'

'No, I wouldn't,' replied Jane firmly.

'But you're not happy, are you, love?' sighed Lyn. 'The sparkle's gone out of you since you moved in with him, and most of the time you're jumpy and on edge.'

'I'd be a fool to deny that it isn't easy sharing a house with and working in the same company as a man whose avowed intention is to get you out of both,' she admitted. 'But what alternative have I? If I move out of the house he'll only switch all his concentration to getting me out of my job.' Her expression hardened. 'It's a job I happen to love and one I've worked hard to get where I am in—and I've no intention of giving it up just because Daniel Blake can't stomach his grandmother's having righted a wrong perpetrated by his grandfather all those years ago.'

'I can—only at a pinch, mind you—understand his wanting you out of the house,' sighed Lyn, 'but not out of the business. I mean, it's not as though you've tried interfering with the status quo, which you could if you really wanted to. Heck, all you're asking is to stay on in your old job!'

Jane gave a small shrug—the mystery of Daniel's attitude to her continuing in her job was one she had given up trying to unravel what now seemed like an age ago.

'Would you like some pudding?' she asked Lyn.

Lyn shook her head. 'That was wonderful, but I couldn't manage another mouthful. . . I've love an Irish coffee, though, if you'll have one too.'

Jane smiled and agreed.

'So—what tactics has he devised in order to get you out of the house?' Lyn demanded the instant the waiter had taken the order.

Jane hesitated, her heart plummeting as she felt the tell-tale colour rush to her cheeks—something she knew Lyn's quick brown eyes would have picked up in an instant.

'He's not. . .' Lyn almost choked. 'Heavens, Jane, he's not stooping to. . .well, to sexual harassment!'

'Of course he's not,' hissed Jane, her cheeks now flaming. 'Lyn, you've a voice like a foghorn at times!'

'But it's something along those lines,' pounced Lyn, her voice dropping to a stage-whisper. 'I can tell it is by your face!'

'For heaven's sake, Lyn,' protested Jane, her eyes widening in complete bewilderment as Lyn suddenly began chuckling softly to herself.

'And, knowing you, you're handling it all wrong. I bet your response is the "how dare you?" ice-maiden routine—which is playing right into his hands,' chortled Lyn weakly. 'What you have to do is turn the tables on him and respond. Heck, Jane, that shouldn't be too difficult—the man's physical perfection personified!'

'And where exactly is that supposed to get me?'

demanded Jane, experiencing a mixture of guilt and relief that Lyn had got it so completely wrong.

'I've a hunch that our beautiful Danny Boy could end up falling like a ton of bricks for you,' stated Lyn, ignoring Jane's dumbfounded look. 'I've always thought what a fabulous couple you'd make, you're both so——'

'I hate to interrupt these fantasies of yours,' murmured Jane stiffly, 'but the odds are well and truly stacked against such an event. . .so where would that leave me?'

They were interrupted by the arrival of their coffees, and Jane found herself praying Lyn's attention would be permanently distracted—it was a subject that was making her feel jittery and ill-at-ease.

'I wonder what the odds would be on your falling in love with him,' said Lyn quietly.

Jane opened her mouth to make a withering reply, then closed it. She took a couple of sips of her drink.

'One way or another, you haven't really much option but to play the odds. . .not that I'd rate them as low as you seem to,' murmured Lyn eventually.

'And which odds are these?' demanded Jane, startled by the harsh defensiveness in her tone.

'The ones on his falling in love with you. . .because you, it seems, are already more than halfway towards loving him.'

When Paul French rang her late the following day and eventually asked her to dine with him that evening, Jane agreed with alacrity. She agreed, not because she had detected no hint of anything lovelorn in his tones—though it was something that relieved her greatly—but because the words with which he had preceded his invitation had startled her immensely.

Time and again she found her concentration drifting towards those words as Paul regaled her throughout the meal with hair-raising tales of his journalistic exploits abroad in the year since she had last seen him. Yet it wasn't until they were on their coffees that she mustered the courage to broach the subject.

'I meant to ask you,' she exclaimed, as though the thought had only just occurred to her. 'How on earth did you come to hear about Dolly Blake's will?'

His strongly defined eyebrows rose fractionally above shrewd grey-blue eyes.

'It was in all the papers,' he replied, then laughed suddenly. 'I haven't been cut off from civilisation, you know—I still read the odd paper or five daily!'

'It's just that I didn't see anything,' muttered Jane, mystified. 'I probably just missed it.'

'It depends what you read,' he replied, curiosity creeping into his look. 'It didn't exactly hit headlines, but it was in all the financial reports. . .which, of course, you should be perusing avidly, now that you're a high-powered executive.'

'Of course I'm not!' exclaimed Jane dismissively, unsettled by the now open curiosity on his face as he leaned back in his chair, looking tanned and lithe and, she had to admit, more attractive than she had ever remembered him. 'I just came into some shares,' she added for good measure, and wished she hadn't when it came out sounding heavily protesting—the last thing she needed was Paul's thinking he was on to a story!

'Fifty per cent share in one of the most powerful businesses in Europe,' he stated, a look she remembered coming over his face and one that reminded her of how she had never been able to reconcile herself to the dedicated ruthlessness with which he would pursue what he considered a good story—no matter what it might cost others.

'You could start playing God if it took your fancy,' he stated, as though thinking aloud.

'I suppose I could—if I wanted to kill the goose laying the golden eggs,' she replied, while inwardly telling herself not to be so ridiculously paranoid—there *was* no story. 'Fortunately, all I want is to get on with my own job and let the experts run the business.'

'So all the reports were at pains to make clear,' reflected Paul. 'Obviously no one wanted the profitable Blake Enterprises boat rocked.' He gave a sudden grin. 'But what about the family feud between the Blakes and the Marleys—aren't you tempted to twist the knife. . .just a little?'

'For heaven's sake, Paul, all that was generations ago!' exclaimed Jane with a dismissive little laugh. 'I'm afraid there's no story to be had anywhere in this—and anyway, you're in foreign affairs now.'

'A story's a story,' he laughed. 'And your getting half the house seems to have all the right ingredients for a really juicy one: a beautiful woman and a man rumour has it women swoon over in their droves, brought by fate under the same roof.' He spread his hands expressively.

'Sounds like a great story,' agreed Jane, forcing a smile to her lips. 'Except for the fact that Daniel Blake—good-looking though he admittedly is— simply isn't my cup of tea, and neither am I his.'

'And who *is* your cup of tea, Jane?' he enquired, a wry edge to his words.

Jane shrugged, maintaining her light-hearted smile. 'I'll let you know when I meet him. And what about you—have you met anyone on your travels?'

'Perhaps—perhaps not,' he murmured, glancing down at his watch. 'I suppose it's time we thought about getting you home—you being a working girl.'

Jane nodded, trying to hide her relief—she had found the past few minutes heavy going, but that had probably far more to do with her suddenly paranoid imagination than her companion, she admonished herself.

'It's been good seeing you again,' she told him as they left the restaurant. 'And the work obviously agrees with you—I've never seen you looking so fit and well.'

'I've got quite a bit on while I'm back,' he said, opening the car door for her. 'But I hope we can do this again—soon.'

'I hope so too,' said Jane, a twinge of guilt warming her smile. This totally uncharacteristic jitteriness of hers was entirely Daniel's fault—he was the one who had had her convinced that the company would take a financial nosedive if news got out of her holding in it. And now she learned it had been in the financial Press anyway. . .as she should have realised it would be, had she had the sense to stop and think about it—anyone who wanted could apply for a copy of a will.

'I believe it's somewhere off here, isn't it—your palatial new home?' enquired Paul minutes later, bringing to an abrupt halt Jane's bloodthirsty thoughts as to what she would like to do to Daniel Blake.

'Yes—just take the next right, then the first left.'

'I must say I'm curious to see if it's as sumptuous as I've heard,' murmured Paul, his casual words throwing Jane into a state close to panic.

'Actually, it's in the most awful mess,' she blurted out, trying desperately to get a grip on herself. 'We've had workmen in for almost a month, putting in a new kitchen. Just about everything that could go wrong has done.'

'But it is inhabitable, isn't it?'

'Yes, of course it is—why do you ask?'

'It's just that, having picked you up from Lyn's place, I wondered if you'd been staying there.'

'Oh, no; I just happened to be going round there this evening and thought it would save time if you picked me up there,' she lied. Her decision to meet him at Lyn's flat was one she had yet to explain fully to herself, she remembered with a twinge of frustration. 'This is it,' she said a few moments later and found out exactly why she hadn't met him here, as her heart plummeted steeply at the sight of Daniel's car in the drive.

Drawing up beside the BMW, Paul switched off the engine, leapt out and opened the passenger door.

'I can think of a few places I'd pass up for even an eighth share in this place,' he murmured, following Jane up the steps to the door as she searched in her bag for her keys while trying to make up her mind whether or not it was absolutely necessary to invite him in.

She had just located the keys, having decided it would look distinctly odd not to ask him in, when the front door opened and Flynn bounded out to give her what had become his customary ecstatic greeting.

'Hello, darling, did you miss me?' she asked, stooping to greet the dog while her eyes studiously avoided the tall figure framed in the doorway.

'I don't know about Flynn, but this darling certainly missed you,' Daniel greeted her almost accusingly. 'They've finished the kitchen and——'

'Daniel, I'd like you to meet Paul French,' she cut through his words as she straightened. 'Paul—Daniel Blake,' she added, then found herself mentally cringing as the two men eyed one another for several seconds before shaking hands with all the warmth of two combatants about to do battle to the death. . .something intuition had warned her might happen.

'None of the equipment in that damned kitchen works,' growled Daniel, completely ignoring the man whose hand he had just so perfunctorily shaken.

Jane flashed him a tight-lipped look of censure, then turned to Paul. 'It looks as though I might be able to offer you a cup of coffee after all—do come in.'

Paul French gave a barely perceptible shrug, then shook his head, his expression one of derisory amusement.

'I think I'll pass the offer up—until you've sorted out the workings of the new kitchen, anyway,' he murmured. 'Goodnight, Jane; it's been great seeing you again after all these months.'

Before she had any idea of his intention, he reached over and cupped her face in his hands, then kissed her full on the mouth.

'Nice to have met you,' he nodded towards Daniel, then turned and left them.

'Would you mind closing the gates after you?' bellowed Daniel after him, then scowled down at Jane before disappearing back into the house.

Almost beside herself with rage and humiliation, Jane stormed inside after him, Flynn close at her heels, neither of them giving so much as a glance at the car turning out of the drive.

'I don't think I've ever witnessed such an ill-mannered display!' she flung at him, her fury spilling over into her words. 'And to think that I've never been anything other than civil to the women you have drifting in and out of here!' Physically flawless, confidence-sapping women; and each giving the appearance of having either stepped out of the pages of a high-society magazine or off a screen. 'Goodness, I even went so far as to make tea for a couple of them because you're incapable of boiling a kettle!'

'I'm perfectly capable of boiling a kettle—the kettle's about the only thing I can get to work in this bloody kitchen,' he snapped. 'And, considering that I'm almost passing out with hunger, I thought I was extremely civil to your little friend. . . Fancy a cup of coffee?'

'Little—he's almost six feet, for heaven's sake!' shrieked Jane, immediately flinging herself down on a chair with a groan of disbelief as the childishness of her words reverberated mockingly in her ears.

'Because if you do—fancy some coffee, that is—I'll make it while you have a look at that cooker. If you manage to get it working, I'll have a steak.'

Jane leapt back on to her feet with a gasp of outrage. 'I'm not your damned housekeeper! I. . . Oh, hell, what's the use?' she muttered, exasperation dousing her anger like a dash of iced water. She marched over to the gleaming new built-in cooker. 'Where are the instructions?' she demanded.

'I wasn't aware there were any,' he replied unconcernedly, filling the kettle. 'I'll make enough coffee for us both as you seem so loath to let me know whether or not you want any.'

Jane opened the top drawer of one of the units next to the cooker—in it she found a stack of brochures relating to the new appliances.

'Heavens knows how, but you've managed to put both the ovens on automatic timer!' she exclaimed witheringly after a few minutes' perusal of the instructions.

'That's all gibberish to me,' he responded with no trace of embarrassment.

Jane readjusted the timing mechanisms.

'But there's absolutely nothing wrong with the hot-plates—all you have to do is touch the relevant panels to turn them on.'

'Where are the knobs?'

'There aren't any!' she exclaimed exasperatedly. 'Can't you understand? All you have to do is——' She broke off with a gasp of alarm as his hands descended on to her shoulders.

'You know, I just can't seem to make up my mind which I'm the hungrier for—you or a steak,' he murmured, his lips against her hair.

'Oh, for heaven's sake, just get me a steak and I'll cook the wretched thing for you!' She would quite happily offer to cook him a multi-course banquet if that were the only way she could get him to move away from her and give her body respite from the dizzying throb of excitement now pounding through it.

'I told you—I haven't decided——'

'Daniel!'

'What?' he murmured, his hands sliding slowly downwards, their pressure firm against the breasts leaping to instant tautness beneath their passing touch. His hands moved on till they finally crossed against her body, pulling it back against his.

'I don't want you bringing other men here,' he muttered, so indistinctly that for an instant she wondered if she had misheard.

He shifted position slightly, then began rocking gently back and forth on his heels, their bodies swaying as one.

'I'm glad you didn't object to my saying that——'

'Didn't object?' croaked Jane, barely able to get the words out as she fought to resist the almost overwhelming desire to turn in his arms and to taste the passion of his mouth on hers. 'I'm too flabbergasted to be able to string a coherent objection together! You, who parade women in and out of here, have the nerve to——'

'I didn't bring them here with the express intention of making you jealous, I——'

'Jealous!' The word came out more stunned than indignant.

'But I hope every one of them made you feel as jealous as I did tonight when you turned up with that guy!'

Without his body to keep hers upright Jane felt she would have ended up a crumpled heap on the floor— he had just told her that the sight of her with Paul had aroused feelings of jealousy in him. . .and thereby reduced her to jelly.

'Is it a deal, Jane?' he demanded huskily as she tried to come to terms with her own, decidedly uncharacteristic reaction to his admission. 'No more men for you—no more women for me.'

'Daniel, I. . .' Suddenly panicked by what was being wrought on her mind and body, she made a violent effort to free herself. 'I don't care if you bring a whole army of women here!'

'I'm only being honest!' he exclaimed, spinning her round to face him. 'You should try the same!' He pulled her against him, the force of the movement flinging back her head till there was no escape from the dangerous darkness gleaming in his eyes. 'I want you so much it's becoming almost an obsession,' he whispered, his hands sliding down her back and spreading against the curve of her buttocks.

'No!' she pleaded in a soft, strangled gasp, her eyes closing as her head began moving from side to side as though in denial of her body's violently erotic response to the savage message of desire emanating from the virile body moulding seductively to hers.

'Put your arms round me, Jane.'

She shook her head, her hands sliding up against his chest to push him away, yet continuing on to cling against his neck.

'Now kiss me.'

She screwed her eyes tightly shut, but this time

she was incapable of shaking her head for the weight of confusing thoughts holding it immobile. Lyn was wrong. . .she wasn't merely halfway to loving this man, she told herself as her lips parted to receive his and revelled drunkenly in the unbridled passion their eager surrender evoked.

The first time she had seen him had marked the exclusion from her life of all other men as potential loves. It was as though, from that moment on, she had been marking time. . .waiting for the seed so haphazardly planted within her to blossom into love.

'Jane, I can't go on like this,' he protested impassionedly against her mouth. 'About the only time I'm free of you is in my sleep—and even then there's no guarantee.'

Her hands rose, stroking against the surprisingly silken thickness of his hair as feelings of indescribable elation staggered drunkenly through her.

'Until I get you out of my system, there's no way I can even begin to consider getting on with my life.'

Her hands froze, her mind uncertain of the words it had hoped to hear, knowing only that these were not the ones.

'Getting on with your life?' she echoed dazedly.

'Setting about finding myself a wife and having a family,' he murmured, his lips searching coaxingly against hers.

Jane turned her head sharply away from the mind-dulling magic of those lips. 'Why the rush?' she asked, a terrible waiting stillness in her.

'I can't say it's a rush, but I am thirty-two come my next birthday. It's something we both have to consider.' He drew back from her slightly and gazed down at her, inscrutability replacing the desire fading from his eyes. 'You have read the small print, so to speak, in my grandmother's will. . .that if either of us dies without heirs both the house and the business in their entirety go to children of the other?' He paused, emitting a harsh laugh. 'Well, well. . .so Jane omitted to read the small print, did she?'

'So it would appear,' said Jane with brittle calm, only just managing to utter the words before something shattered explosively within her.

With an almost trance-like lack of conscious volition she drew back her hand and hit him across his face with every ounce of strength she possessed. And, still caught in the timeless weightlessness that accompanied dreams, she saw his head recoil, as though in slow motion, with the impact of the blow and slowly turn back.

His arms released her, dropping to his sides.

'You should thank your lucky stars you're a woman,' he intoned, his voice devoid of expression. 'And just remember that the next time I hold you in my arms like that there will be only one possible outcome to it.'

CHAPTER FOUR

LETTING out a soft groan of exasperation, Jane picked up the telephone ringing beside her on her desk.

'Sorry, Jane, but Danny Boy's just rung to say he wants you up in his lair,' came Lyn's apologetic voice. 'Preferably about thirty seconds ago, judging by his tone. Also, another couple of board documents have just been delivered—thick ones!'

Jane's hand tightened painfully on the receiver.

'Jane?'

'I'm counting.'

'Is it helping?' asked Lyn with a sympathetic chuckle.

'I doubt if counting up to a million would help,' sighed Jane. 'Perhaps I'll try a coffee instead.'

'Good idea—I've a pot on the go.'

'You're an angel, Lyn; I'll be with you in a tick.' Jane replaced the receiver and, with an exclamation of loathing, pushed aside the pile of documents littering her desk, then rose and marched from her office.

'Coffee's poured,' Lyn greeted her. 'But what about Danny Boy?—he stressed it was urgent.'

'He'll just have to wait,' replied Jane mutinously.

Lyn gave her a slightly anxious look, then handed her a mug.

'Here, have this; and sit down and relax,' she ordered, 'before you blow a fuse.'

Jane sat down, her face tense. 'Lyn, this isn't fair on you,' she protested. 'You've had to carry my workload as well as your own for the past few days.'

'And when it gets too much for me you'll be the

57

first to hear,' responded Lyn easily. 'But is it really all worth it—from your point of view?'

'There's a meeting of the full board of directors tomorrow!' Jane exclaimed indignantly.

'Yes, and magnanimous Danny Boy's been showering you with all the relevant documents,' stated Lyn wryly.

'Because I asked him for them!'

'Jane, I know the full board doesn't get together that often, but hasn't it occurred to you that it would take them the best part of a month—sitting full-time—to discuss in anything approaching detail that load Danny Boy's been dumping on you?'

'Of course I realise most of it will be dealt with summarily——'

'So why on earth are you going through it all as though you're about to be minutely examined on every aspect of it?'

'Lyn, I have to understand what's going on,' protested Jane, puzzled and a little hurt by her friend's attitude. 'Surely you understand that?'

'No—I'm afraid I don't,' replied Lyn quietly. 'You're attempting the impossible. And it annoys me to see you fall right into Danny Boy's hands like this. He's swamping you with all this unintelligible paper-work because he knows you're pig-headed enough to try ploughing through it!'

'I *have* to try!' exclaimed Jane hotly. 'I'm the one who demanded the seat on the board. . . I was under the impression you agreed I had every right to!'

'And so I do,' retorted Lyn. 'Jane, you and Danny Boy own the company between you—but you're the personnel officer and he's the managing director! The man has degrees in structural engineering and chemistry—and half a dozen other subjects, for all I know. What I'm trying to point out is that he was probably

weaned on what you're attempting to digest over-
night. . . Jane, you're aiming for the impossible!' She
broke off with a groan of frustration. 'This is crazy—
why are we having a slanging match over this, of all
things?'

'Quite frankly, I feel like tipping the rest of this
coffee over you,' muttered Jane, then gave a wan
smile. 'Because the awful thing is—you're right.
Most of those papers could have been written in
Serbo-Croatian for all the sense they make to
me. . .but what am I going to do?' she wailed. 'Lyn,
do you realise I haven't even the vaguest idea what
format these wretched meetings take, let alone anything else?' She placed her mug on the desk and
jumped to her feet. 'I'll just have to go and tell Daniel
I shan't be taking my seat on the board.'

'Jane, all I was trying to do was get you to be
realistic about all this,' protested Lyn. 'Of course you
don't have to chuck in your seat on the board. Go
along, listen to what they say and accept that you'll
probably not understand ninety per cent of it.'

'You really have decided to take on the role of my
mother, haven't you?' chuckled Jane.

'It's hard to believe I'm nearly two years younger
than you,' grinned Lyn. 'It must be. . . Oh, heck!'
she groaned, as the phone rang on her desk. 'Danny
Boy!'

'I've gone,' exclaimed Jane. 'And thanks for the
lecture—Mother, dear,' she teased, and dashed from
the room.

Though he called out when she knocked, Daniel was
on the telephone when Jane entered the room.

He glanced up and motioned her to be seated, an
expression of scowling impatience on his face as he
made several exasperated attempts to get a word in.

He swung his chair slightly as Jane sat down, a

movement that brought his profile sharply into her line of vision, and with disastrous effect.

This isn't just crazy, it's downright unhealthy, she railed against herself, her pulses racing out of control as her body outrageously relived the intoxicating sensation on hers of the mouth now uttering words into the mouthpiece. Yet when he fell silent, his fingers tugging impatiently against his bottom lip as he waited to speak again, it was the breath-stifling eroticism of his teeth biting against her own lower lip that flooded into her mind.

How could she possibly imagine herself to be in love with a man like this? She barely knew him and what little she did she found loathsome. What had he, apart from his looks? He was just about the most unpleasant person she had ever had the misfortune to——

'There were a couple of things I wanted to discuss with you,' he announced, scattering her thoughts as he flung back the receiver. 'Firstly—that new typist.'

Jane's hackles rose instantly, any thought of love ousted by the phrase 'jumped-up typist' leaping tauntingly to her mind.

'Which new typist?' she asked. 'I've just taken on two.'

'Not for my section, you haven't,' he informed her brusquely. 'But if there are two of them, that should simplify matters—you can swap mine for the other.'

'But they were placed in the positions most suited to them,' protested Jane. 'And I've had no complaints from Jacky.'

'I'm not interested in my secretary's opinion, quite frankly.'

'No—you wouldn't be,' snapped Jane before she had a chance to bite back the childish retort.

'And, if you must know, Jacky's been up to her eyeballs with some highly confidential work for me—

the sort of thing that couldn't be entrusted to a typing clerk,' he informed her icily. 'And, because she's been otherwise occupied for the past few days, I've been left to the tender mercies of your new recruit.'

'It's hardly fair to expect any new employee— especially a typing clerk—to step into your secretary's shoes, surely——?'

'You misunderstand me,' he interrupted, his tone almost reasonable. 'It's not her work I'm complaining about. It's other little things—such as the way she always leans against me whenever she places something on my desk. . .or stretches across me, her blouse undone practically to her navel.' He gazed across at her, his eyes gushing innocence. 'The problem is, I can hardly keep my hands off her.'

For the briefest of instants, Jane felt as though she had been punched savagely in the stomach.

'I'll see what I can do about making a switch,' she eventually managed.

'Good,' he murmured, leaning back in his chair as his eyes coolly raked her. 'You're more distraction than I can handle right now as it is. . .and I'm sure you don't want the field cluttered up with rivals.'

'If that's all,' stated Jane frigidly, getting to her feet, 'I'll get back to work.'

'No—it isn't by any means all,' he informed her, rising and walking round to where she stood. 'So sit down,' he ordered, placing both hands on her shoulders and pushing her back down on to the chair she had just risen from. 'Good,' he murmured, then sat down before her on the desk-top.

Jane closed her eyes and, in a monumental effort to regain control of herself, began counting in earnest. Had she not done so she would have been back on her feet, telling this obnoxiously arrogant bully exactly what she thought of him; and then telling him she had no intention of spending so much as another minute in either his house or his business. . .which was exactly what he was hoping she would do.

Once she felt the temptation was safely behind her, Jane opened her eyes once more and found them looking up into a mocking, dark-lashed gaze of vivid blue.

'What is it that you've resisted with such difficulty: dealing me a crippling left hook or storming out of here—preferably for good?'

'The former,' she retorted instantly. 'The latter is something I'll never give you the satisfaction of doing.'

'So—what dissuaded you from your customary violence?' he gibed, plainly amused.

'Your looks, Daniel,' she informed him with saccharine sweetness. 'As they're about all you've got going for you, I didn't think it fair to deprive you of them.'

His eyes flickered coolly over her.

'Perhaps that's something we should discuss in more depth, one of these days,' he reflected with a chilling, almost threatening softness, before slipping back to his feet and returning to his chair. 'But right now there are other matters to be dealt with, such as whether any of the papers have contacted you regarding the contents of my grandmother's will.'

Jane gave him a startled look. 'They haven't.'

'Well, they have me. I had hoped the coverage by the financial Press would have been the end of it— unfortunately I've started getting calls regarding it from the less savoury sections of the Press. . .gossip columnists, judging by the inanity of their questions.' There was hostility in the eyes that met hers. 'I merely wondered if you had been similarly pestered.'

Jane returned his look with equal hostility.

'As I said—I haven't,' she informed him. 'But, if I do, I shall take great pleasure in telling them just how well you've adjusted to the changes in your life. . .and, of course, of the methods you're employing in your attempts to get me out of the house, not to mention the company.'

'You can tell them whatever you choose,' he informed her in that same softly threatening tone, 'just as long as what you say has no repercussions—none whatever—on this company.'

'I would say that's entirely up to you,' she told him, her tone matching his. 'All you have to do to ensure the stability of your precious business is to face reality and accept that I've no intention of leaving either it or the house.'

'And you intend aiding my facing that reality with a spot of blackmail, is that it?' he asked with a sneering laugh.

'Daniel, what name would you give to what you've been trying on me for these past few weeks?' she asked quietly.

There was the pallor of fury on his face as he rose swiftly to his feet.

'You're on very dangerous ground——' He broke off with an angry oath at the sound of a knock on the door. 'Yes?' he snapped as the door opened.

'Sorry—I didn't realise you had anyone with you, Daniel.'

Jane's eyes widened in disbelief at the unfamiliar husky softness in a voice she only just recognised as that of Joan Sellers.

'You asked to see these proofs, but if now isn't a convenient time. . .'

'Yes. . .sorry, Joan, it completely slipped my mind!' exclaimed Daniel, glancing down at his watch. 'Would you mind giving me another five—perhaps ten—minutes?'

'Not at all,' came that soft, co-operative and barely recognisable voice, followed by the sound of the door closing.

'Right,' he stated, glowering down at Jane. 'Let's recap on a few facts, shall we? My wanting you out of the house and the business still stands. . .as does my intention to employ whatever methods necessary to achieve both. So whatever, if anything, you decide to say to the Press, choose your words with extreme caution—or be prepared for the consequences.' He picked up a folder from the desk and flung it across to her. 'And have a read through that—or, better still, get your solicitor to explain it to you. Once you've understood it, we can get it properly signed and witnessed.'

There was undisguised suspicion in the glance Jane gave the folder lying on her lap.

'It's not going to bite you,' he drawled. 'It's merely a document similar to the one my grandmother signed after the death of my father and grandfather. It simply gives me the executive control I've always had over your half of the company. The shares, naturally, remain yours, while you become. . .' he broke off, his expression faintly amused '. . .a sleeping partner, so to speak.'

Jane grasped the folder, rose to her feet, and hurled it across the desk at him.

'I think you know what you can do with this,' she informed him angrily, and marched to the door.

'Talking of sleeping partners,' came his voice from so close behind her that Jane nearly leapt out of her skin, 'I do hope you're suitably impressed by how assiduously I've been sticking to our agreement. . .though I can't say this enforced celibacy agrees with me.'

'I've told you, I don't give a damn how many women you have!' retorted Jane, her cheeks flaming even more hotly as she realised how ambiguous her words had been. 'And, for your information, I shall be bringing a friend back this evening!'

She wrenched open the door before he had any chance to react, and almost walked smack into Joan Sellers.

'Sorry—I was just about to knock.'

'Don't apologise,' snapped Jane, then hastily forced a smile to her lips as she stepped past the woman. 'He's all yours.'

And you're welcome to him, she added to herself, consumed with fury as she stormed through Jacky's empty office.

'It's fabulous. . .it really is,' breathed Lyn, as she and Jane deposited several carrier-bags of shopping on the kitchen table.

Jane glanced around the discreet magnificence of the designer-built kitchen with a slightly jaundiced eye.

'And so it should be after all the time and hassle——'

'I didn't mean the kitchen particularly!' exclaimed Lyn. 'It's. . .it's just the whole place!'

Jane smiled at her friend's unbridled enthusiasm. 'All you've seen is this and the hall,' she chuckled. 'Why don't you go and have a browse around while I get these put away?'

'Great!' said Lyn, making straight for the door, then turned as she reached it. 'You know, I can't understand how you can seem so. . .so utterly blasé about all this.'

'I can assure you, I don't feel in the least blasé about it,' said Jane, slightly thrown by the remark. 'Anyway, off you go and let me make a start on the meal.'

Setting aside what she needed, Jane put the rest of

her purchases away, then began emptying the dishwasher.

Perhaps Lyn had a point, she pondered with a frown; though blasé wasn't exactly the right word for what was often her total lack of consciousness of the elegant opulence of her new surroundings. Yet she had always loved beautiful things, she puzzled as she began tackling the vegetables—and there was little about this house that could be described as less than beautiful.

'You know, you could really throw the party to end all parties here,' announced Lyn on her return, her enthusiasm undiminished. 'Those two fabulous rooms—the ones with the dividing doors. . .with them opened out you'd have what almost amounts to a ballroom!'

'Perhaps you should suggest it to Danny Boy,' teased Jane, covering the food she had prepared.

'Which reminds me,' said Lyn. 'Where is he? And Flynn—I'm dying to meet him!'

Jane gave a half-shrug, though her pulses leapt with apprehension. 'I'm not sure. . .he's probably taken Flynn for a walk.'

'But he is eating with us, isn't he?' asked Lyn.

'To be honest, I forgot to ask him what his plans were,' replied Jane, her spurious claim to honesty causing her to colour slightly. 'As I'm only doing steaks, there's no problem whether he turns up or not.'

'No,' agreed Lyn, a noticeable lack of certainty in her tone. 'Jane. . .it won't cause problems, my being here? I mean, you did rather ask me on the spur of the moment.'

'Lyn, of course it won't!' exclaimed Jane, the odd niggle of guilt that had been flaring up in her ever since issuing her somewhat ulterior invitation to Lyn

now rearing insuppressibly within her. 'Come on—
I'll show you around upstairs.'

She hadn't exactly *said* it was a man she would be
bringing back, she argued with herself as she led Lyn
from room to room. No, but she had most certainly
implied it, countered her integral honesty as they
eventually reached her bedroom.

'Oh, Jane, it really is lovely. . .so bright and airy
and elegant. And such a view!' she exclaimed, walking to the window. After a while she turned, her
expression unsmiling. 'I must be driving you mad,
oohing and aahing like a visitor to a stately
home——'

'Lyn, of course you're——'

'I didn't mean to sound critical,' interrupted Lyn
anxiously. 'In fact, critical is the last thing I feel. . .but
you're definitely not getting the thrill out of this place
you would have done under normal circumstances,
are you?' she asked sadly.

Jane sat down on tbe bed, shaking her head
defeatedly. 'No,' she sighed. 'I can't claim that I am.'
She gazed slowly around the beautiful room that was
now hers. 'You and I come from the same sort of
backgrounds, Lyn—good, solid, ordinary homes.
And you're right—under normal circumstances, I'd
be over the moon having the chance to live in a place
as beautiful as this. But as things are. . . Lyn, I just
don't seem able to feel anything much about it.'

Lyn sat down beside her on the bed. 'And I can't
have helped matters much,' she muttered guiltily.
'Jane, that remark I made the other night about your
being practically in love with Danny Boy—it was an
idea that hadn't really occurred to me until it just
popped out, but. . . Jane, are you?'

'Sometimes the pessimist in me almost has me
convinced I am,' replied Jane, the candour of her
own words both surprising her and bringing her a

feeling of relief. 'To be honest, I've always found him incredibly attractive.'

'Tell me something I hadn't already guessed,' murmured Lyn with a teasing grin.

For an instant Jane looked aghast, then gave a rueful chuckle. 'But how?'

Lyn shrugged. 'I don't really know. Intuition, I suppose, because you weren't exactly giving anything away. . .though it was Danny Boy's eyes that gave *him* away on one particular occasion that springs to mind.'

'Lyn, he flirted with me now and then, that's all!'

Lyn gave a small, non-committal shrug. 'So tell me, what does the optimist in you have to say about your feelings for him?'

Jane pulled a face. 'That I'm probably suffering from a dose of infatuation. . .that I'm far too level-headed to let myself fall in love with a man who could behave with the cold-blooded ruthlessness Daniel is capable of.' She broke off with an exclamation of disgust. 'Lyn, you'll not believe it—he's actually forbidden me to bring any men back here!'

'Perhaps he wants you all to himself,' chuckled Lyn.

'It's not funny,' protested Jane. 'There are times when I find him so infuriating that. . . Oh, heck, I suppose I might as well be completely honest,' she groaned. 'I'm pretty sure he thinks you're a man. Lyn!' she exclaimed frustratedly as the girl dissolved into a fit of the giggles and buried her head against the pillows. 'For heaven's sake. . .what I meant was that he probably thinks the person coming to dinner is a man. You see, when——' She broke off with a cry of alarm as the bedroom door swung open and Flynn bounded in. 'Hello, darling,' she gasped, as the dog placed his front paws on her lap and began licking her face in ecstatic greeting.

'Flynn, down!' ordered Daniel from the doorway.

'Oh. . .hello!' gasped Lyn, dragging her face from the pillows. 'I've come to dinner. . . I hope you don't mind.'

For the barest fraction of an instant, the man in the doorway seemed to freeze to the same stillness as his dog sitting at Jane's feet and gazing up at her from adoring eyes.

'Mind?' he murmured, his smile stunning as he strolled into the room and came to a halt beside his dog. 'I'm delighted to hear it, so how about some introductions? Lyn, meet Flynn.'

The dog gazed up at his smiling master, as though for confirmation, then he offered Lyn his right paw.

'Oh, you darling!' crooned Lyn ecstatically, nearly knocking Jane off the bed in her eagerness to shake the proffered paw.

With that social chore behind him, the dog returned his gaze to Jane and offered her his paw. She took it, startled by, and desperately trying to ignore, the inexplicable lump that the delightfully spontaneous gesture had brought to her throat.

'It seems Flynn doesn't want Jane to feel left out,' observed Daniel with wry amusement. 'And I thought you were supposed to be a one-man dog, Flynn.'

'Except that Jane's a woman!' exclaimed Lyn, then gave a squeak of disbelief as she realised what she had said.

'Why—so she is,' murmured Daniel, his words accompanied by a look of utter guilelessness. 'So tell me, what are we giving our guest for supper?'

We? Our? Jane glared at him, trying vainly to convince herself it was only for Lyn's sake she wasn't ordering him out of her room.

'Steak, new potatoes, fresh peas and salad,' she

chanted, rising to her feet. 'I'll go and put on the potatoes.'

'While Lyn and I get Flynn his supper,' grinned Daniel, the customary mocking in the eyes meeting Jane's.

'Flynn and Lyn,' chuckled Lyn. 'I hope neither of us gets confused.'

But there was plenty of confusion in Jane, caused by the welter of unsettling thoughts racing through her head as she prepared the meal with the sound of Lyn's and Daniel's exchanges in the background.

He was at his most relaxed and charming as he went out of his way to make Lyn feel welcome—not that it took much to put someone as relaxed as Lyn usually was at her ease, thought Jane with a mixture of affection and envy. But what she was finding more confusing and unsettling, as she listened to their increasingly easy banter, was the difficulty she was having conjuring up the cold-blooded ruthlessness in him that should make loving him an impossibility. His relaxed charm was something she was unlikely to be on the receiving end of, she reminded herself angrily, hastily suppressing the vivid memory she suddenly had of that day, almost four years ago, when he had dashed into the lift behind her.

'Would you like me to lay the table?' offered Lyn.

'It's all right, I'll see to the dining-room,' said Daniel, before Jane had a chance to reply. 'But if you follow me, you can bring in some plates from there to be heated, if you like,' he added.

Jane put on the steaks, surprised that he had selected the dining-room—with its cabinets displaying dauntingly priceless-looking dinner services—in which to eat; it was a room to which he had once referred as a mausoleum and he normally seemed to prefer to take his meals anywhere other than in it.

But it was in the dining-room they ate, the three of

them seated in isolated splendour at one end of a table that could probably have seated twenty with ease.

It was much later, when they had retired to the elegant splendour of the main drawing-room, that the thought occurred to Jane that the evening had turned out to be a disaster—simply because it had gone so incredibly well.

Though Daniel had probably never exchanged much more than the odd polite word with Lyn in the time she had been in his company's employ, he was now responding to her amiable personality with spontaneous warmth and charm.

If she was having such difficulty reminding herself what an arrogant monster this apparent epitome of charm could be, she thought miserably, what chance was there of Lyn's ever realising the implacable harshness that lay beneath that fatally engaging surface?

With feelings of envy she was powerless to suppress, she listened to the laughing exchanges of the couple on the sofa as their darkly gleaming heads bent over an album of photographs of Flynn—one she had no idea existed until Daniel had produced it on Lyn's request to see a picture of the dog as a puppy.

'I don't think I've ever seen anything more adorable,' bubbled Lyn, reaching down to stroke the dog sprawled at their feet. 'And you've grown up to be the handsomest boy I've ever seen too,' she informed him.

'I have to agree with her there, Flynn,' chuckled Daniel, giving the dog a pat as he rose and returned the album to the bureau from which he had taken it. 'Which is just as well, otherwise poor Danny Boy might have resented such competition.'

'Oh, heck!' groaned Lyn, flashing a mortified look

towards Jane, who suddenly found herself fighting laughter.

'I hear you give a great rendition of "O Danny Boy",' grinned Daniel, returning to the sofa.

'He didn't hear it from me, I promise you,' protested Jane through her laughter, as Lyn subjected her to a look of murderous outrage.

'Good heavens, it's gone midnight!' exclaimed Lyn, resorting to looking at her watch in order to avoid the amused gaze of her employer. 'I'd better ring for a cab!'

'I've a much better idea,' murmured Daniel sweetly. 'I'll drive you home and you can serenade me on the way.'

'What. . .me? Sing?' groaned Lyn.

'That's the deal,' grinned Daniel.

Lyn was still trying every trick in her repertoire to get out of her side of the deal as the front door finally closed behind them and left Jane feeling acutely alone in the sudden silence surrounding her.

With Flynn by her side, she cleared away the dishes and stacked the dishwasher, wondering why she should start feeling so alone now when she had, in effect, felt isolated throughout the entire evening. Her contribution to the conversation had been the minimum required of her and not a word more.

With Flynn darting in and out with her, his tail wagging contentedly, she checked the rooms and switched off lights.

'Time for your bed, old fellow,' she told him, unconsciously using his master's term of endearment.

The dog followed her into the utility-room and obediently climbed into his basket, his tail thudding happily against the wicker as Jane knelt down beside him and put her arms round his neck.

She felt a terrible, aching sadness fill her as she

rested her cheek against Flynn's golden coat. Something had always held her back from loving and fully appreciating this beautiful house. . .an instinctive part of her that had always accepted the inevitability that the day would come when she would have to leave.

'But it couldn't stop me growing to love you, old fellow,' she whispered brokenly. . .nor the man who would one day bring about her inevitable departure.

CHAPTER FIVE

'WELL you seem to have made quite a hit with the directors,' observed Daniel, strolling into Jane's office as she prepared to leave. 'That's probably because, like me, they tend to appreciate a woman who knows when to keep her mouth shut.'

And, apart from introductions, she hadn't opened hers once throughout the entire protracted meeting, thought Jane bitterly, studiously continuing to tidy her desk as she resolved not to rise to the proffered bait.

'My, you're doing a thorough job on that desk,' he drawled. 'You're not by any chance clearing it in readiness for your successor, or would that be too much to hope for?'

Jane slammed shut the drawer, anger and frustration burning hotly within her. If only Lyn could hear her precious Danny Boy now, she thought resentfully, she would probably have difficulty believing her ears. But Lyn, together with the rest of the Blake Enterprises staff, had left for home almost an hour ago.

'The fact that I can appreciate a woman keeping her mouth shut when necessary doesn't mean to say I like them dumb,' he murmured, obviously determined to goad her into response.

'No? I think you'll find you'd have preferred me dumb once I start opening my mouth,' she informed him coldly, then picked up her bag and jacket.

'The Press have been on to you at last, have they?' he enquired mildly.

'They don't have to be. I have all the access I need

to the Press in Paul French; now, if you don't mind,
I'd like to lock up.'

He obligingly stepped out into Lyn's office, his
cool blue eyes unnervingly scrutinising her every
movement as she locked the door of her office.

'As long as you keep it in mind that he's not
welcome at the house,' he mocked, then paced
impatiently to the outer door. 'The security staff can
deal with that—leave it.'

'If you're in a hurry, go—I'm quite happy getting
a bus,' she muttered. She rarely had a lift with him,
either in the morning or evenings, as he tended to
keep long and often erratic hours.

'I'm here, so we might as well travel home
together—besides, there's something we need to
discuss.'

'Which is?'

'Your signing your executive rights over to me.'

Jane flashed him a look of pure loathing and made
to walk straight past him.

'Oh, no, you don't, young lady,' he snapped,
grabbing her by the arm and bringing her to a sharp
halt. 'I've had enough of this! Have you any idea at
all of how many people worldwide depend on this
company for their livelihood? Or perhaps you consider your mindless preoccupation with your ridiculous family vendetta more important than the
livelihoods of large numbers of people!'

'You're the one who's mindless and ridiculous if
you think that,' she protested, perplexed by the
undisguised fury in the eyes blazing down into hers.

'Needless to say, you have no idea of the convo-
luted nature of this company's charter. . .which now
demands I get ratification from you on just about
every policy decision I make, unless you legally
waive your rights.'

'And what on earth has that to do with people's jobs?' she demanded, angrily shaking free her arm.

'Your refusal to empower me to continue running the company as I always have can only mean that you intend interfering.'

'Daniel, how many times——?'

'Whether it's your intention or not, sooner or later the company would grind to a virtual halt. It runs as smoothly and profitably as it does now because I don't have to waste my time justifying my decisions to those who wouldn't have the first idea what I was talking about anyway.'

Jane looked at him in complete horror, neither willing nor able to believe he could consider anyone, let alone her, capable of such tortuous malevolence. He spoke as though he actually believed her only goal in life was to avenge her grandfather, no matter what the cost. Which only went to show what sort of values the Blakes had, she thought in disgust.

'Well?' he demanded harshly.

Shaking her head in disbelief, Jane hitched the strap of her bag higher on her shoulder. 'I'll sign the wretched thing,' she informed him icily. And with decided reservation, she informed herself bitterly, almost certain she had just been subjected to a neat piece of emotional blackmail—no one in his right mind could seriously claim to believe the rubbish he had just spouted!

'Good, I'm glad that's settled—now perhaps we can go home.'

Jane followed him through the building to the underground car park in complete silence, doubt and indignation gnawing angrily away at her.

'I've decided it would be best to get it all signed and done with this evening,' he announced abruptly, as they drove from the car park.

'Why—because you're afraid I'll go back on my

word?' demanded Jane. 'That might be the sort of thing you'd stoop to, but I certainly wouldn't. But, as my word clearly means nothing to you, you'll just have to sweat it out until Monday and see what happens then.'

'OK, we'll leave it till Monday,' he muttered, weaving the car into the traffic with an aggressive ruthlessness that brought her heart to her mouth.

Jane leaned back against her seat and closed her eyes, letting her mind drift back over his confounding accusations, the result of which was a swift rekindling of anger and disbelief in her.

'Only a complete fool could possibly believe I intend to harm the company!' she exclaimed in a sudden bitter rush.

'How should I know how your mind works?' he retorted indifferently, taking a corner at a speed that brought a squeal of protest from the types. 'But one thing I'm sure of—had our roles been reversed and I were the one sneaking into the company under an assumed name——'

'I did no such thing!'

'The only motive I could possibly have would be vengeance.'

'Perhaps you should stop judging me by your appalling standards,' retorted Jane as he got out of the car and opened the gates.

'Perhaps I should,' he replied, slipping back in and driving the car to the house, where he brought it to a screeching halt in a flurry of gravel. 'But I'm surprised you bother wasting your advice on me—since you regard me as nothing more than a pretty face.'

He had leapt from the car and up the steps and had the front door open by the time Jane had finished digesting his words. And, by the time she entered the house, he was romping like an overgrown schoolboy on the stairs with Flynn.

'What are we having for supper this evening?' she called out on her way to the kitchen. 'I might as well get a start on it.'

The sound of her voice brought Flynn racing to greet her with a yelp of delight.

'Did you think I'd abandoned you, Flynn, coming home so late?' she chuckled as he almost bowled her off her feet with the enthusiasm of his welcome.

'You didn't ask me to get any shopping,' stated Daniel, half-heartedly trying to remove dog hairs from his suit as he entered the kitchen.

'It's your job!' exclaimed Jane exasperatedly.

'Make up your mind—you got it yesterday.'

'Only because Lyn was coming round.'

'How was I to know you weren't getting it today? You didn't leave me a list or say anything.'

'For heaven's sake!' exploded Jane. 'Aren't you capable of doing a bit of shopping without my having to write you a list?'

'What else do you expect?' he drawled, strolling over to the sink and filling the kettle. 'I'm only a pretty face.'

'That's the second time you've dragged that up this evening,' observed Jane coldly. 'I'm surprised an ego as inflated as yours is so bothered by it.'

'I told you at the time you made the remark that I'd like to discuss it further with you,' he drawled, ladling coffee into the cafetière. 'The idea of there being women around who are attracted by the male equivalent of the dumb blonde fascinates me.'

'Daniel, what are we going to do about food?' she demanded impatiently.

'There are such things as restaurants, you know,' he replied, switching off the kettle and pouring water over the coffee grounds with meticulous attention. 'And stop using that tone of voice—you're upsetting Flynn.'

Caught off guard by the unexpectedness of such a remark, Jane glanced over at the dog who had retrieved one of his innumerable soft toys from the utility-room and now lay stretched out on the tiled floor with his cheek against it.

'He always produces Teddy when he feels upset, don't you, boy?' continued Daniel in tones of cloyingly tender understanding.

'This is ridiculous—I really am beginning to believe you *are* a half-wit!' groaned Jane, picking up her bag and jacket and storming towards the door.

'And to think I was banking on it being a case of "love my dog, love me",' his drawling words followed her. 'Needless to say, if you don't like the way things are here, you're always welcome to leave.'

And leaving was a temptation she was finding more and more attractive, Jane realised defeatedly as, with trembling hands, she impatiently shed her clothes and stepped under the shower.

There was a cold ruthlessness in Daniel Blake that her every instinct warned her could easily degenerate into naked cruelty, given the right circumstances. She had been aware of a similar streak in at least two men she had come across, both of whom had also been exceptionally attractive—though, to be fair, that was probably coincidental, she decided hastily. But she hadn't been in the least attracted to either—on the contrary, she had been repelled by what she had detected in their characters.

She stepped from the shower, wrapped herself in a towel and began combing through the heavy wetness of her hair, a vulnerable hopelessness etched on her features.

She could dwell on Daniel Blake's numerous faults for ever and a day, but nothing would alter the fact that there was a side to him that embodied all the

softer attributes necessary to counteract the harshness in him. . .even if it was a side he seemed
inclined only to show to his dog!

She gave a bitter laugh, conscious that there was
little for her to be laughing about as she made her
way back to the bedroom. It was her glimpses of that
side of him with Flynn and, admittedly, with Lyn
last night, that had led to her downfall. With a sigh,
she made for the window, an expression of spontaneous tenderness lighting her face as she spotted
Flynn at the far end of the garden, pouncing playfully
on the apples that had fallen from one of the trees.

She really ought to collect up those fallen apples
and do something with them, she was telling herself,
when the dog suddenly began letting out blood-
curdling yelps of agony, leaping up and down and
shaking his head frantically.

She had raced from her room, down the stairs and
through the house, and was halfway across the
immaculately striped lawn before becoming fully
aware of her panic-stricken dash.

'What's happening to him?' she shrieked at Daniel,
who, having virtually rugby-tackled the yelping dog,
had brought him to a halt in his arms. 'Is he having
a fit?' she cried as she saw Flynn paw frantically at
his mouth.

'No, but he soon will be if you don't stop that
hysterical racket,' snapped Daniel, heaving the dog
across his lap. 'Try to hold him still for me,' he
ordered, grasping Flynn by the jaws and prising
them open.

Jane sank to the grass beside him and flung both
her arms round the struggling body.

'It's all right, old fellow,' Daniel soothed softly, 'I
just want to have a look.'

The dog's body stilled to no more than a tremble.

'Hell, with all these wasps around, he's managed

to get stung by a bee!' muttered Daniel, releasing Flynn's jaws, then picking him up in his arms. 'Poor old lad, we'll get you inside and see if we can get that nasty sting out,' he crooned tenderly. 'There's a first-aid box in the utility-room,' he called over his shoulder to Jane, who had struggled back to her feet and was now trying to secure the towel around her. 'Would you mind getting it? There should be some tweezers in it.'

'But shouldn't we take him to a vet?' asked Jane, having to mince along behind him, thanks to her over-tight readjustment of the towel.

'If we can't get the sting out, I'm afraid we'll have to,' he replied, striding through the veranda doors, Flynn still cradled in his arms. 'Though you won't like that, will you, old fellow?' he murmured. 'You always howl the place down because it reminds you of having jabs.'

Jane fetched the first-aid box from the utility-room and opened it out on the kitchen table, while Flynn, now sitting with his head trapped between his master's knees, whimpered pathetically.

'Poor boy,' she murmured, stroking his head.

'Have you the tweezers?' demanded Daniel impatiently.

She nodded.

'Right—I'll get his mouth open while you see if you can remove the sting.'

Jane gave him a startled look.

'You'll have to get down by my knee,' exclaimed Daniel, prising Flynn's mouth open the moment she complied. 'See that swelling—just behind his front teeth to the left?'

'I can't see a thing,' protested Jane.

'For goodness' sake—lean over and look. . . Stay, Flynn!'

Ducking her head under one of his arms, she

leaned across a muscled thigh and peered into the dog's open mouth.

'Can you see it now?'

'Yes—and the sting right in the middle of it,' she exclaimed. 'It's all right, darling, I shan't hurt you,' she whispered nervously, then reached into the dog's mouth and gently removed the sting at her first attempt. 'Got it!'

With a loud sigh of relief, Daniel spread his knees to free the dog and sent Jane sprawling backwards on to the floor.

'Flynn, get off!' she begged, as, his ordeal behind him, he pounced delightedly on the end of her towel and began wrestling it from her. 'Flynn!' she shrieked, one hand attempting to hold the top part of the towel in place while the other played tug of war for the bottom end. 'Daniel, stop him, for heaven's sake!' she yelled as she felt herself being pulled across the floor by the towel.

'Don't be such a spoil-sport,' protested Daniel. 'He's bound to need a little playful distraction after what he's been though—isn't that so, Flynn?'

'Daniel!'

A strong, darkly tanned hand reached over and covered hers.

'What shall we do—count to three then pull?' he enquired lazily.

'Tell him to let go, damn you!'

'But he's enjoying himself——'

'Daniel!'

'OK, Flynn, drop it!' he commanded, and the dog instantly obeyed. 'Come on, let's get you a bowl of ice-cubes to munch on,' he added affectionately. 'It won't make up for Jane's unkindness to you, but it might help your mouth.'

Scarcely believing her eyes as she witnessed him tipping a mound of ice-cubes from the freezer into

Flynn's drinking-bowl, Jane got gingerly to her feet. She gazed down in confusion at the rumpled towel around her, hugging it to her and not daring to readjust it in case she lost it completely.

'Well, I really do think the least you could do is give him a bit of a pet, after all he's been through,' Daniel informed her piously.

The movement purely reflex, Jane made to reach out to the dog crunching noisily on the ice-cubes, then returned her hand to the slipping towel with an exclamation of frustration.

'I'm afraid I don't share your infantile sense of humour,' she informed him tartly as he laughed softly to himself.

'Humour, infantile or other, has nothing to do with my desire to see you minus that towel,' he informed her in softly mocking tones. 'I'm merely displaying perfectly healthy male impatience in wishing to glimpse the body that will soon be mine anyway.'

'You are just about the most arrogant——'

'Before you start screeching abuse at me,' he murmured placatingly, strolling to her and taking her lightly by the shoulders, 'I should point out that my body will also be yours to do with whatever you will—within the bounds of reason—for the duration of our affair.'

'Daniel, will you please let go of me?' hissed Jane, unable to take any action herself for fear of dislodging her towel.

'You don't seem to be putting up anything of a struggle, my silken-skinned Jane,' he mocked, his hands lightly caressing her naked shoulders. 'Is that an indication of your weakening resolve?'

'You know damned well I can't struggle,' she accused, terrified that the excitement that had begun coursing through her body the instant his hands had touched her was now flamboyantly manifesting itself all over her skin.

'Didn't anyone ever tell you there's no such word as can't, Jane?' he taunted huskily, drawing her towards him and lowering his head till their lips all but touched. 'No—don't do that.'

'Do what?' she demanded through clenched teeth, her eyes closing tightly.

'Close your eyes. . .you always do that whenever I come too close. And then you start waging that battle with yourself which you invariably lose.'

Though fully aware it was merely an empty gesture of defiance, she opened her eyes, allowing them to rise no higher than the firm line of his jaw while she frantically tried to work out whether or not the pulse running amok at her throat could possibly be out of his line of vision.

'You can relax, Jane: I've no intention of putting your will-power to any test right now.'

Her eyes flew to his and whatever it was he detected in them brought an expression of amusement to his face before he abruptly released her.

'I think a good run in the park might take Flynn's mind off what he's been through—don't you?'

Jane nodded. It was a purely reflex physical reaction performed by her body while her mind metaphorically scraped itself from the floor. She had never, in her entire twenty-three years, come across a man even remotely like him—one moment practically seducing her and the next consulting her over the welfare of his dog!

'You see, I thought that, as we've no food, we could kill two birds with one stone—give Flynn his run and grab something to eat in the park.'

'The food isn't the greatest here, but at least you can eat outside when the weather's as it is now,' remarked Daniel, as they drank coffee after their meal. 'There don't seem to be any places around where you can eat with a dog in tow. . .though I suppose I could always try passing him off as my guide dog, if the need ever arose.'

Jane flashed him a slightly startled look—neither by the tone of his voice nor the expression on his face could she gauge whether he was joking or serious. He had to be joking, she reasoned bemusedly, because no man who could seriously talk in terms of pretending he was blind in order not to be separated from his dog would have handed him into the custody of two young boys as Daniel had earlier done, and without any discernible qualms.

'Don't you think you ought to check where those boys have got to with Flynn?' she asked, her memory jogged by her bemused thoughts.

'Mark and Jonathan? They'll be back in their own good time,' he replied nonchalantly. 'They often wander off with him. Poor little devils have spent all their lives in a flat where animals aren't allowed.' His face brightened noticeably. 'But they told me the other day that they're moving soon and their parents have promised them a Flynn of their own.' He gave a soft chuckle. 'They always refer to him as though he were a breed.'

'Have you always had a dog?' she asked, her even tone belying her appalled awareness of the inexplicable rush of tenderness those casually uttered words had churned up in her.

'I had another dog once. . .when I was a child,' he replied, something indefinably alien in his tone which the almost jerky abruptness with which he suddenly raised his cup to his lips seemed only to emphasise. 'And you?' he demanded when he had drained his cup. 'You seem to get on well with animals—or dogs, anyway.'

'I had a cat when I was very small,' she said, her gaze skimming the hard, lithe body on the seat next to hers. In jeans, a white T-shirt and leather trainers, it was a body that still managed to exude that same air of almost arrogantly self-assured authority it did when dressed in the finest Savile Row could produce. Yet she somehow sensed a ripple beneath that surface cool. . .that she had inadvertently touched an extremely raw nerve. 'I can barely remember that cat. And, as my stepfather is allergic to animal fur, Jenny—my stepsister—and I couldn't have pets.'

'More coffee?' he asked, disconcerting her by gazing into the far distance as he spoke, rather than at her.

'Thanks,' she replied, the feeling that his customary cool had been ruffled only increasing when he gave a waiter the order and then returned to gazing ahead of him without his eyes ever once contacting hers.

'Did you get on with your stepfather?' he asked, much to her surprise.

'Yes—in fact, I love him dearly. He's one of the kindest, most decent men you could hope to meet.'

It was then that his eyes did meet hers, the glint of antagonism she found in them startling her with its complete unexpectedness.

'Dolly—my grandmother—seemed to have got it into her head that your life had more or less been ruined by your grandfather's misfortunes.' His look was now openly hostile. 'Obviously she got it all wrong,' he added dismissively. 'Ah, good—here's the coffee.'

Jane speculated briefly on what might have happened had the waiter's presence not provided her with those few moments in which to temper the volatility of the rage suddenly possessing her—and then she rounded on him.

'So, you don't think a child's life could be ruined when its parents' marriage is destroyed by bitterness?' she asked, her tone soft with suppressed anger. 'I was a baby when your grandfather cheated mine out of all he and my father possessed! I was three when my mother, a woman of incredible inner strength and vitality, finally broke under the strain of finding the man she loved reduced to a stranger so eaten away by bitterness he seemed hell-bent on drinking himself to death.'

'And did he?' asked Daniel, with a brutal candour that took her breath away.

'No,' she replied, almost rejoicing in the feeling of pure hatred his words elicited in her, a hatred encompassing the judgemental smugness in him that could never conceive of the anguish and remorse that had later engulfed her father and which had stayed with him probably until the day he had died. 'Probably the most terrible thing about it all is that my father wasn't one of life's pathetic weaklings—and you needn't think I'm saying that out of any reluctance to believe ill of my own flesh and blood. It was what he had previously been that made his virtual disintegration so inexplicable. . .and nearly destroyed my mother.'

'As you say, such a reaction does seem pretty odd,' he conceded, the barest trace of sympathy entering his tone. 'If either were to go to pieces, the older man should have been the more likely candidate—it's easier for a younger man to start all over again. Though, from what I've heard of Joe Marley, he could have done it with ease, had he chosen.'

Jane shifted uncomfortably on her chair. 'My mother once told me she felt my grandmother's death was the real trigger; she died barely a month before they lost the company, and my father was exceptionally close to her.'

'And his relationship with your grandfather?'

Jane felt herself tense as that and other questions began resurrecting in her mind—questions that had nagged at her over so many years, but which she had always left unasked for fear not only of the answers they might have evoked, but also from an instinctive protectiveness towards her mother.

'They never spoke again.' She hesitated, frowning. 'But I honestly don't know what that stemmed from—my grandmother's death, or your grand-father's swindling them——'

'The fact is, your grandfather gambled away the business,' he cut in sharply. 'And I mean that liter-ally. My father and grandfather had to hock them-selves up to the eyeballs to raise the money to buy back the parts of the company Joe Marley had delib-erately sacrificed to the roll of the dice.'

Jane gave a bitter laugh. 'You Blakes will swallow anything, no matter how ludicrous,' she accused, 'as long as you don't have to face any unpalatable truths!'

'And you know what those truths are, do you?' he demanded.

Jane picked up her cup and drank from it, unwill-ing to risk her expression betraying what could only have been a lie.

'I'm the last person to claim my grandfather was any saint; but he and Joe Marley were two of a kind. The business empire they created was, odd though it may seem, no more than a by-product of the devious games of intellectual one-upmanship they played against one another over all those years.'

'That still doesn't alter the fact that your grand-father cheated mine out of——'

'For God's sake, face up to the facts, can't you?' he exclaimed impatiently. 'It was all or nothing with those two, and ultimately one had to win and the other lose. They used the company like a chess piece, for heaven's sake! It was my father's realisation that he could end up in a position identical to the one in which your father found himself that led him to having the present watertight charter drawn up for the company.'

'I'm surprised your grandfather let him,' snapped Jane, appalled by the strength of the bitterness their conversation was dredging up in her. Yet it was a bitterness evoked solely by shadowy half-truths formed in her mind over the years, and based less on knowledge than on the odd snippets she had managed to pick up and piece together. Yet now she was beginning to understand that it was this terrible bitterness from which her mother had tried to protect her over the years. And she knew with certainty that her mother had meant it when she had declared the past to be no longer relevant to their lives and had urged her to take the job with Blake Enterprises if that was what she really wanted. . .yet, of all those concerned, it was her mother who had probably paid the highest price.

'He let him because, without the stimulus of Joe Marley, he needed something into which he could channel all that intellectual energy of his. And it was because he happened to channel that energy into the company that it's become the powerful organisation it is today.'

'So the Blakes all sailed happily off into the sunset,' she exclaimed bitterly, 'while the Marleys were left with their lives in ruins!'

'I'm surprised, given how passionately biased you are about the whole matter, that you didn't revert to your true name,' he observed coolly. 'And, since you're obviously one of those people who deludes themselves that wealth is the bringer of happiness, your income from the company should provide you with a fair bit of such happiness. However, were you to sell me your half of the house, you might find yourself almost delirious with joy—it's an exceptionally valuable property.'

'One can, I believe, have too much of a good thing—thanks all the same,' she replied, her attempt to mimic that infuriatingly languid drawl of his not quite succeeding. 'But, speaking of delusions, am I really to take it that all that Blake wealth didn't actually bring you happiness. . .that it was a heart-wrenching case of poor little rich Danny Boy?'

'I'm afraid your timing's all wrong, pussy-cat,' he informed her with a coldly humourless smile. 'That's the sort of question you'd be best advised to put off asking till you share my bed.' He broke off to wave to the two boys coming into view with Flynn prancing at their heels. 'And even then there's no guarantee you'll get an answer.'

CHAPTER SIX

THE tension in the atmosphere between them was so acute by the time they arrived home that even Flynn seemed to sense it. He prowled disconsolately from room to room, seeking out first one, then the other of them, dividing his time between them and obviously unsettled.

He had last parted from Jane in her bedroom to seek out Daniel once again, this time in the drawing-room.

When the rippling notes of a piano had first begun floating up to her, Jane had assumed Daniel was playing records. Only gradually had she realised that those faultlessly beautiful sounds were coming from the magnificent grand piano in the drawing-room.

That Daniel played at all came as a surprise to her; though that was possibly because he had never once, to her knowledge, been near the piano since she had moved into the house. That he played the instrument so well that her ears had for a while accepted they were hearing a professional recording astonished her.

And her astonishment only went to show just how little she knew about him, she thought edgily as she descended the stairs, the brilliantly executed magnificence of the music in her ears only increasing the lethargic melancholy sapping her spirit.

She felt a desperate need to see her mother; to hear her softly reassuring voice answering all those questions that had remained unasked over so many years.

'Hello, old fellow; would you like some supper?' she asked Flynn as he glided into the kitchen after her, sitting himself down as she turned towards him and offering her his paw.

She took the paw, then sank to her knees beside him, putting her arms around him.

'You've had a bad enough time of it as it is today, without our making it worse by confusing you like this,' she sighed, tears suddenly welling in her eyes. 'Oh, heck, what on earth's happening to me?' she choked, as the tears spilled over and coursed down her cheeks. 'Come on, let's get you fed.' She rose, scrubbing furtively at her cheeks with the back of her hand.

Her mother was right, she tried desperately to convince herself; the past was far behind them and had no place in their present lives. . .and it would be nothing more than selfish indulgence on her part to attempt dragging it all up.

'Go and get your bowl, Flynn, there's a good boy,' she urged, getting out a tin of dog-food and opening it, while her mind censoriously demanded to know why it was she still hadn't got around to writing and telling her mother of the incredible contents of Dolly Blake's will.

'Oh—you're doing it.'

With a small start Jane glanced up to find Daniel in the doorway, Flynn at his side with his bowl between his jaws.

'He summoned me from the drawing-room,' continued Daniel, his smile wryly affectionate as he glanced down at the retriever. 'Decided you wanted us both dancing attendance tonight, did you?'

'Maybe he just feels in need of a little extra attention after his ordeal,' murmured Jane, giving her face a surreptitious wipe as she stooped to get the dog-biscuits out of a cupboard. 'Come along, Flynn, let's have your bowl.'

Both man and dog arrived at her side.

'He's over his ordeal,' stated Daniel, that familiar mockery lacing his tone. 'He's simply an incurable romantic—he doesn't like us being at war.'

'I wasn't aware that we were,' replied Jane crisply. 'Come along, boy,' she added, then took the bowl outside to the patio.

'That doesn't say much for your powers of observation,' remarked Daniel from behind her.

'Slow down, Flynn. Anyone would think you hadn't been fed for a week,' she chided, ignoring those words and having her own ignored in turn by the dog.

'Why have you been crying, Jane?' he asked, his tone curious rather than sympathetic.

She gave a small shrug—there was obviously nothing to be gained by denying it.

'The mere fact that you ask shows that you'd probably never understand, not even in a million years,' she informed him coldly, walking past him and back into the kitchen.

'It's rather difficult to understand when you know as little as I do about the whole affair. . .as little as I suspect you do.'

'At least you had the benefit of your grandmother's letter—surely that must have explained things?'

'Not really—though I'm quite happy to let you know the relevant parts of it. . . Would you like some tea?'

'Yes. . .please. Daniel, I'd be most grateful if you would tell me what your grandmother said.'

'Did you know she was once engaged to be married to your grandfather?' he asked, switching on the kettle.

'Yes—but only because Mr Watson, her solicitor, told me.'

'Well, apparently it wasn't until she'd got herself

engaged to him that she realised it was my grandfather, Robert, she loved. It seems that Robert had
always been in love with her and, devious devil that
he was, he was always scheming to win her from
Joe.'

Jane set out the cups, hanging on to his every
word.

'Dolly had told no one of her change of heart, but
it was round about that time that Robert arranged to
have Joe compromised by one of the local beauties.
Dolly, who wasn't above a bit of scheming herself,
took the opportunity of breaking off the relationship,
even though she knew Joe to be completely
innocent.'

'What a horrible thing to do!' exclaimed Jane.

'Oddly enough, she did it like that out of compas-
sion. She knew Joe well enough to realise that losing
her because of a foolish misunderstanding would be
far less damaging to his pride that losing her to
Robert.'

'But she *married* Robert, for heaven's sake, so Joe—
I mean, my grandfather—must have realised.'

'That's just the point—he didn't,' replied Daniel.
'It was only when Joe had given up all hope of ever
winning her back and had started seeing your grandmother that Dolly started showing her true feelings
towards Robert.'

'That must have taken ages,' gasped Jane, a grudg-
ing respect growing in her for the unknown Dolly
Blake. 'And talking of ages—what happened over
the company must have taken place almost thirty
years later.' She broke off, frowning. 'Yet Mr Watson
was under the impression that both were connected.'

'And so they were, to a large extent,' muttered
Daniel, bringing the tea to the table and joining her.
'In fact, it's difficult imagining two grown men carry-
ing on the way our grandfathers did. But it seems

that all those years later Robert, in a fit of pique, boasted to Joe about how he had set him up over Dolly. . .and then all hell was let loose.'

'But couldn't Dolly—I mean, your grandmother—have explained?'

'The fact is, she tried. But he refused to believe her—not that you could really blame him after the act she'd put on all those years before.'

'Perhaps not,' sighed Jane, then exclaimed impatiently, 'But did it really matter—after almost thirty years?'

'One way or another it mattered desperately to Joe, because it was from that day on that he set about systematically destroying the company.'

'What do you mean—systematically destroying it?' demanded Jane. 'You told me he'd gambled it away.'

'Same thing—it doesn't do a multi-faceted business much good when its most vital parts are more or less used as chips at the gambling tables. I'd say that was a pretty swift way of destroying it.'

'But they were in partnership! He couldn't possibly——'

'He could and did,' snapped Daniel. 'The pair of them owned everything between them—yet the whole set-up was so appallingly loosely structured that either one of them could have frittered away the lot without so much as a signature from the other being required. Though it would have been interesting to see what the result would have been had one done so and the other sued.'

'Why didn't your grandfather sue, then,' demanded Jane accusingly, 'once mine alledgedly started losing great chunks of the business?'

'Because it wasn't his style,' he retorted sharply. 'Just as it wouldn't have been your grandfather's, from what I've heard of him. If you don't pour that tea now, it won't be worth drinking,' he added irritably.

Jane was on the point of telling him to pour it himself when she guiltily remembered that it was he who had made it.

'Anyway, he played Joe at his own game and eventually got control of the lot.'

'Well I don't care what you say,' she muttered defiantly. 'My grandfather would never have behaved so irresponsibly to his own family. . .his own son.'

Protest though she might, she could detect the doubts niggling in her mind spilling over into her words. She had only got to know her grandfather after her own father's death—and even then she couldn't claim to have known him all that well, though, as children often were, she had been enthralled by his outrageous eccentricity. But the only words she had ever heard him utter regarding the Blake-Marley affair had been on the occasions when he had got monumentally drunk, and then he had raged in incoherent passion against the treachery of his erstwhile partner. The thought that now came to her was that the loss of the business he had helped build from scratch had never once been specifically mentioned in those rambling diatribes. Could it really have been Dolly over whom he had felt so cheated, and not the business?

'Yet you say his own son never spoke to him again,' pointed out Daniel.

Jane took a sip of her tea, her confused thoughts veering off at troubling angles.

'I also said that I didn't know what caused that,' she replied, her tone edgy. 'And one thing that should be remembered is that my grandmother died round about the time all this had flared up. . .for all anyone knows, it could have been grief over her death that triggered off his bizarre behaviour.'

'And your father's too?' enquired Daniel sceptically. 'One would have expected him to support his widowed father in their shared grief—not cut him out of his life. And certainly not to behave so badly that his wife leaves him.'

'My mother didn't leave him,' blurted out Jane defensively. 'He was the one who left us when it began getting through to him just how his behaviour was affecting my mother.'

'How noble of him.'

'How dare you sneer?' she rounded on him bitterly. 'You didn't even know——'

'Look, I'm sorry—I had no right to make a remark like that,' he apologised without hesitation. 'Jane, the point is that you can hardly claim to have known him yourself—yet you seem hell-bent on sanctifying someone who caused your mother such pain. You were—what—ten when he died?'

'Yes.' But she *did* know him, she protested silently. She knew and loved the man who had started writing to her weekly when she was eight and had continued doing so right up until the day he had died in a traffic accident far away in Brazil, the country to which he had gone when he had left her and her mother. 'But I loved him. . .and I've a feeling my mother went on loving him too, right up until his death.'

'Which can't exactly have been a bundle of fun for your stepfather,' he observed.

'I'm sure life wasn't exactly a bundle of fun for either him or my mother for several years,' reflected Jane. 'Ted, my stepfather, was my mother's doctor; his wife, whom he adored, died soon after the birth of their daughter. My mother and he might have married for reasons other than love initially, but it came to them eventually.'

And how she and Jenny had delighted in watching their respective parents fall deeply and almost frivolously in love, she remembered wistfully. And what inner security that love had brought to her mother—enabling her to allow Joe Marley into their lives once again, so that he could get to know his only grandchild.

'They were lucky; love seems to be a very rare commodity,' remarked Daniel, rising abruptly. 'My parents split up when I was little more than a toddler—I probably hold some sort of record for the number of stepmothers and fathers the pair of them managed to provide me with over the years—perhaps it was love they were looking for.' He cocked his head to one side and gazed down at her, his expression closed. 'Who knows? My mother may even have found it—she's lasted longer with this latest husband of hers than she did any of the others,' he stated, then picked up the cups and took them to the dishwasher, apparently oblivious of the look of shocked disbelief on Jane's face.

'How terrible for you,' she exclaimed weakly.

'Why should the idea of my mother at last finding love be terrible for me?' he queried, deliberately, she was sure, misunderstanding her.

'You know that's not what I meant.'

'I can't imagine what you do mean,' he drawled coldly. 'After all, I lived in this beautiful house and was waited on hand and foot by the best staff money could buy. . .the list is unending of all the happiness that sort of money provides.' He glanced down at his watch. 'There's something I wanted to catch on television, so if you wouldn't mind. . .?' He strode to the door, turning with a sudden exclamation as he reached it. 'There was one thing I meant to mention to you—I'm going away for just over a week on

Wednesday. Shall I arrange for Flynn to go to kennels——?'

'Good heavens, no!' exclaimed Jane in horror, then immediately tried to compose herself. 'I mean. . . I'd love to look after him. . .if you'd trust me to, that is.'

'Where's Flynn's concerned, I trust you implicitly,' he murmured with a small mocking bow. 'Who knows? I might even be obliged to make visiting arrangements between the pair of you once you've left here.'

'Jane, you look whacked!' exclaimed Lyn, leaping up as Jane entered the office. 'Sit down and put your feet up,' she fussed. 'I'll make us some coffee.'

'But you should have packed up and gone home ages ago,' protested Jane guiltily, flopping down on to a chair.

'I wanted to hear how you got on,' Lyn told her, busying herself with the coffee. 'So tell me, did you manage to track down Professor Leigh?'

Jane gave her a look of wry amusement. 'I tracked him down, showed him the report and he rang Daniel at Juan-les-Pins—happy?'

'And what was decided?'

'That Blake Enterprises are not only pulling out of the project, they're going to campaign to have the whole thing halted.'

'Good old Danny Boy, I just knew that was how he'd react!' cheered Lyn.

'Only a monster would react otherwise,' pointed out Jane. 'After reading that latest report, Professor Leigh declared he considered the consequences of such a project going ahead could be ecologically devastating; he's contacting the government about it.'

'But you have to admit there are an awful lot of businessmen who'd have said "to hell" and gone for the profit,' persisted Lyn. 'So tell me, how does it feel to be a fully fledged high-powered executive?' she demanded, handing Jane a mug of coffee.

'Lyn!' Jane groaned out the name in protest. 'Something out of the ordinary cropped up while Daniel was away; he contacted me and asked me to get a copy of a certain report, track down the relevant director, show it to him and get that director to ring him—and that's what I did; no more, no less!'

'Ah, but it was *you* he rang from France, and *you*——'

'Because, with him away, he could hardly ask Jacky to abandon his office and go haring off in search of the elusive professor—that's why. And, besides, I had to sign the letter he and Professor Leigh concocted between them.'

'You see?' exclaimed Lyn triumphantly. 'He's finally accepted you as his partner!'

'Lyn, he accepted my authority to sign on behalf of the company because it suited him,' she pointed out wearily. 'He'd have had to interrupt his holiday and come back here otherwise.'

Lyn looked so crestfallen that Jane found herself wondering what her expression would have been had she learned of the woman Daniel had taken on holiday with him.

She pressed the mug hard against her lips in a vain effort to suppress the memory of the violence of the stomach-churning sensations that had assaulted her—and had gone on doing so intermittently ever since—that morning only two days ago when, having left earlier, Daniel had returned to the house to collect something he had forgotten, a Titian-haired vision of perfection in the passenger-seat of his car.

'I suppose you're right,' sighed Lyn, then began sipping her drink morosely.

'Cheer up,' chivvied Jane, able to force lightness

into her tone as the immediate ferocity of those memories began to ease a little. 'Isn't this the weekend you and John are off to that jazz festival?'

Lyn nodded, her face brightening fractionally. 'Why don't you come with us? I'm sure John would be able to arrange another ticket!'

'And one for Flynn?' smiled Jane, shaking her head. 'It's very sweet of you, but Flynn and I plan to——' She broke off, her eyebrows rising questioningly as a tap on the door was followed by the sound of its opening.

'Oh, there you are, Jane—I thought I heard voices.'

Jane swung round in her chair at the sound of that familiar voice. 'Hello, Joan. What are you doing around so late?'

'I've been trying to get hold of you all day, but you didn't appear to be answering your telephone. It's funny the way so many people's working hours seem to shrink the moment the boss goes on holiday.'

Jane felt her hackles rise, as they invariably did sooner or later in the presence of Joan Sellers.

'I was out—on business, as it happens,' she stated evenly. 'And it must be something terribly urgent that you need to see me about if it keeps you at the office this late.' She heard the edge that had crept into her tone, but she had had to comfort far too many others who had suffered through this coldly beautiful woman's malicious tongue for her to have any qualms about it.

'Actually, it wasn't business at all,' murmured Joan, a tight little smile accompanying her words. 'I was wondering if you had Daniel's telephone number in France.'

Having heard Lyn's soft intake of breath, Jane studiously avoided meeting her friend's eyes.

'You could have asked Jacky for it,' she hedged—

why on earth would this woman want Daniel's telephone number?

'I specifically didn't want to involve Jacky—you know what gossips secretaries can be.'

Before Jane could open her mouth to defend Jacky, the woman continued.

'Actually, it's Katrina I need to contact—my cousin, if you really must know.'

Jane looked at her blankly.

'The girl he's taken to France with. . . Oops, let's just pretend I didn't say that,' twittered Joan coyly, heading back to the door. 'I've just remembered—there's another friend who'll probably have the number.'

Lyn let out a hissing breath as the door closed. 'I can honestly say that I've never spent more than a few seconds in that woman's company without ending up wanting to go for her throat!' she exclaimed angrily. 'She's trouble; and there are several things about her worrying me right now—such as exactly what all that charade was about and why she should think *you* would have Danny Boy's number——'

'Lyn, by now the contents of Dolly Blake's will is quite likely to have filtered through the grapevine. And the fact that he and I share the same house. . .' She broke off as Lyn shook her head emphatically.

'I think Jacky probably knows, and you know what secretaries are like,' she mimicked savagely. 'Jacky wouldn't breathe a word to anyone. Another thing that worries me is why Joan's so keen to let you know Danny Boy's taken off with one of her tacky relations.'

'I doubt if you'd have described her as tacky if you'd seen her,' murmured Jane wryly. 'She's really rather stunning.'

'You *knew*?' shrieked Lyn.

'Lyn, I've already told you the place is always knee-deep in his women,' she sighed, then silently corrected herself—at least it had been until he had barred her from bringing men there and had decided to impose a similar restriction on himself regarding women. 'He's just that sort of man. . .and, anyway, he's looking for a wife.' She flung up her hands in disgust with herself as those last words just slipped out. 'Lyn, could you just forget I said that? I shouldn't have. It's just that I've had a long day, I'm dead on my feet, and Flynn will be wondering where I am—*and* demanding a walk!'

When she and Flynn arrived at the park, it was with feelings of the deepest gratitude that Jane handed him over to the two young boys so obviously lying in wait for them.

'We had to see him, because we're moving tomorrow,' explained the elder.

'And we're getting our own Flynn,' chipped in the younger. 'But when our little Flynn's big enough we can bring him here to meet big Flynn.'

Jane gave the children money for an ice-cream, a peculiarly lumpy feeling coming to her throat as she remembered Daniel telling her, the night before he had left, that he had first checked with the boys' father before ever having done so.

She flopped down on to one of the benches. . .he had done nothing more than any other intelligent adult would have done, she remonstrated with herself angrily.

She leaned back and closed her eyes, wishing a wind would blow up and lighten the heavy humidity of the mid-September air. Then she began wishing she didn't feel so physically and mentally limp. . .then a few seconds later decided that she could put up with the limpness if only she didn't feel so overwhelmingly miserable. It was at that point that she dispensed with wishing and began grappling with her thoughts—it was as though every time there was a lull in them Daniel would obligingly slip in and fill the gap.

She missed him. Yet had anyone asked her, prior to Wednesday, how much contact they had, living under the same roof, she would have said little. But now that he was gone it was as though there was a gigantic void in her life. . .as though she had been parted from a hitherto constant companion.

The truth was that she had been apart from a companion who invariably addressed her in drawling tones of sarcasm; who wanted her out of his house and his life, and who would use any means, no matter how low, to achieve that. . .and she missed him desperately.

For almost an hour she remained immobile on that park bench, hopelessness dragging her down into a gloomy torpor from which she aroused herself only with considerable difficulty when the boys reappeared with Flynn, accompanied by a petite, laughing-faced young woman.

'I'm Allison Wright—Mark's and Jonathan's mother,' the woman introduced herself with a friendly smile.

'And can we have Dan's telephone number?' begged Jonathan, the younger boy, before Jane could offer her own name.

'So that we can ring him and tell him when we've got our Flynn,' explained Mark.

'Now calm down, boys,' pleaded their mother affectionately, throwing Jane an apologetic look.

'Of course they can have the number,' said Jane, smiling as the elder boy immediately proffered her a note-pad and pencil. 'I'm sure Flynn's going to miss them,' she told their mother as she wrote down the number.

'They'll be back here to see him, don't you worry,' laughed the woman. 'We're not that far from this area, but it's such a relief to have found somewhere they can have a dog of their own. Come along, boys—we've all that packing to finish, so say goodbye to Flynn for the time being.'

The boys flung themselves on to the dog, who licked them ecstatically.

'I don't know where your husband's found the patience to put up with them all these months,' called the mother to Jane as she dragged her reluctant sons away. 'But thanks to you both for being so understanding.'

Her husband, thought Jane, almost savouring the words as she and Flynn strolled home. Tired and mentally off guard, she let her thoughts drift till her mind was filled with images of the Daniel she had first met, yet barely known; a man whose dangerously attractive looks had been softened by laughter and whose eyes had sought hers to caress in teasing flirtation; and, by the time she had let herself and Flynn into the house, she found herself alarmingly close to tears.

'Well, one thing's for sure, old fellow,' she told him shakily, as he presented her with his bowl, 'I can't carry on like this.'

That realisation clung like a limpet in her mind, nagging unceasingly at her over the hours, and remaining with her as she laying tossing in her bed in a vain search for sleep.

There was only one solution and she might as well face it, she told herself wearily; she must start looking for somewhere else to live immediately. . .and swallow the pride that had driven her so recklessly to declare that she would stay put no matter what.

She would start looking tomorrow, she promised herself, vigorously plumping her pillow, then freezing to stillness at the sound of a soft half-yelp of a bark. She sat up and switched on the light, conscious of the prickle of hairs at the nape of her neck.

Flynn often made quite loud noises in his sleep, she reminded herself impatiently—and she was overreacting to being alone in the house. Having just released the breath she had been unaware of holding, she reached out to switch off the light. She snatched back her hand, the unmistakable sound of a closing door choking her with fear.

Scarcely aware of what she was doing, she swung her legs over the side of the bed, the fear trapping the breath in her lungs as the softly purposeful tread of approaching feet seemed to echo in the air around her.

She was imagining it, she shrieked voicelessly to herself, trying to attune her ears, yet unable to for the deafening thud of her pounding heart.

Triggered by the soft rap on the door, it was an unknown part of her that took control, urging her trembling body towards the bathroom with the idea of locking herself in there.

'Jane—are you awake?'

'Daniel!' The name slipped from her in a soft moan of terror, her body slumping weakly against the wall as the door burst open.

'Jane, what's wrong?' he called to her, striding towards her and catching her as she almost fell into his arms.

'I thought. . . I thought. . .' She took a shuddering gulp of air, unable to continue.

'Jane, you're trembling,' he protested, his shadowed cheek rubbing distractedly against hers as his arms tightened fiercely around her. 'I didn't mean to frighten you like that. . . I thought you were asleep until I saw the light under your door.'

'Why didn't you warn me? Why didn't you ring?' she wailed against him. 'I thought you were a burglar. . . I was going to lock myself in the bathroom!'

'Darling, I'm sorry. . . I just didn't think.'

Darling? The word echoed unfamiliarly in a mind still trapped in the stupefying aftermath of fear.

'Why are you here?' she demanded, the confusion brought about by that endearment sharpening the words into accusation.

'Because. . .hell, because I haven't been able to get you out of my mind since the moment I left!' he exclaimed angrily. 'Because I couldn't take being away from you for a moment longer!'

His words only deepening her confusion, she buried herself against him, her arms clinging around him in compulsive fierceness.

'And now I've succeeded in frightening you half to death,' he groaned, his arms tightening bruisingly. 'I'm so sorry.'

'You had that woman with you—so why should you miss me?' she accused him illogically, the words spilling from her unchecked.

'You're jealous!' The words were a half-laughed groan of triumph as his lips began moving against her cheek, down towards hers. 'And I'm glad!' His hands rose and cupped her head, forcing her gaze up to the glittering heat in his. 'How can you possibly be jealous when you've as good as emasculated me as far as other women are concerned?' he demanded, his breath hot and inciting against her mouth as he drew her back into his arms. 'Tell me you've missed me as much as I've missed you!'

'I've missed you!' she exclaimed involuntarily, a strange, trembling eagerness possessing her.

For an instant he seemed to freeze, then his mouth

took hers, his tongue as potent an invasion as the hands that began restlessly exploring the contours of her body, drawing up her nightgown in swift movements of impatience.

'Lift your arms,' he groaned softly against her mouth, drawing the gown off her as her arms rose in instant acquiescence. 'Tell me how much you missed me,' he demanded almost angrily, the sure touch of the hands caressing her body bringing soft gasps of protest bursting from her as her every sense leapt in a fever of excitement.

'I don't want to talk about missing you,' she protested, her words choked and barely coherent as her trembling fingers undid his shirt and tried to force it over his shoulders. 'I hated missing you!' she accused mindlessly, her hands now moving to the waistband of his trousers as he obligingly finished removing his shirt.

'Do you think I got any joy out of missing you?' he exclaimed angrily as he kicked off his shoes and impatiently began assisting her in her clumsy attempts to remove his trousers.

It was only when he had to release her to remove them completely that her befuddled mind began to get a clear picture of what she had been doing—stripping him; as though stripping a man was an activity that came second nature to her!

'Daniel,' she gasped, the realisation restoring her sanity like a slap across the face. 'I think I ought to tell you——'

'How much you've missed me,' he finished for her, his arms impatient as they enveloped her and crushed her body to the naked, urgent heat of his. 'So do I,' he murmured distractedly, lifting her against him and burying his face against her breasts, the impassioned exploration of his lips and tongue scattering any shred of sanity she still possessed.

'Because you've haunted me day and night,' he groaned, lifting her completely and carrying her to the bed.

She clung to him, her body fighting, not for release, but in a fierce desperation not to be separated from his even for the instant it would take for him to lower her to the bed.

'Jane, please,' he protested hoarsely, trying to free his head from the stranglehold of her arms. 'Oh, hell,' he groaned, as her clinging struggles brought his body crashing down with hers. 'Darling, you'll have to try to relax,' he pleaded, the coaxing touch of his hands as they tried to still her writhing body only inflaming her beyond endurance.

'I can't,' she half sobbed, her every action now governed by the savage ache of a need over which she had no control.

'I want to be gentle with you,' he protested, trying to steel his body against the unbridled invitation with which hers now bombarded it.

'Daniel, please,' she begged against the heat of his mouth, sharp ripples of exultation jarring through her as his hands began moving against her body with purposeful sureness, while in the distant reaches of her mind stirred a ghost of a fear of the complete unknown. But it was a ghost held at bay by the compelling drive of the need awoken in her by the swift surge of tension in the body now openly preparing hers for its total possession. And, as though long-practised in the skills of love, her body accepted with eager impatience the purposeful guidance of his, only once losing its reckless assurance in that agonisingly sweet moment of plundering invasion that wrenched the breath from her lungs in a sharp cry of protest.

But it was a moment lost forever as her body strove to accommodate the urgent rhythm of its longed-for possession, only to find itself racked by a series of shuddering explosions that danced in unbearable ecstasy within her before bursting from her in sharp cries of joyous disbelief. And, as she heard her own incredulous joy echoed in his softly groaned laughter, she felt that wild intoxication stir within her and begin taking possession of her once again, until love and laughter rioted exultantly throughout her senses.

But later her laughter deteriorated into soft sobs of protest as her body throbbed in searing desperation, driven by the intense urgings of the body now goading it towards heights she knew could only be unattainable. And it was as the volatile ardency of his invading passion finally erupted, filling her with the molten sweetness of its explosive exultation, that she knew the impossible had been attained. And there was the tender possessiveness of love in her arms as they enfolded the powerful body now lying heavy on hers in the passive, softly shuddering aftermath of loving.

Her mind was still lost in the dizziness of rapture when Jane felt him move then gently ease his weight to his elbows as his eyes gazed down into hers. But it was the total lack of any expression on his face that trapped the ragged breath within her in a swift premonition of fear.

'You're the only woman I've ever known with the capacity to laugh from the sheer joy of lovemaking,' Daniel said, his words expressionless as his features, despite their hoarse breathlessness.

Her mind, striving to cling to its fast-fading joy, reluctantly attempted examining those words, desperately seeking some hint of approval in them as they feared finding accusation.

'I always laugh when I'm——'

He silenced her by placing his hand over her mouth—firmly, yet not without gentleness. 'When you're making love?' he asked, accusation now unmistakable in his tone.

Hurt and bewildered, she turned her head to the side to free her mouth, her feeling of despair complete as his sudden movement severed the last links of the love that had united them. Except that it was only on her part that there had been love, she reminded herself with an empty bitterness, dragging herself upright and hugging her knees protectively against her chest as the savage ache of her desolation threatened to choke her.

'I thought you'd have noticed that's a claim I wasn't qualified to make,' she intoned through frozen lips, the sickening thought that her total inexperience was something he might not have been aware of suddenly overshadowed by the realisation that, this being her room they were in, there was nowhere she could flee.

'Of course I noticed it,' he stated quietly. 'I'm sorry I finished your sentence for you. . . What were you going to say?'

'Not what you thought. . .but it doesn't matter anyway.'

'Jane, I realised too late that this was your first time. I was unable to respond to knowing it. . . I'm sorry.'

Her expression one of bewilderment, she turned to find him stretched out on his back beside her, his hands linked behind his head and his lean, powerful body completely at ease in its glistening nakedness.

'What do you mean. . .you're sorry?' she whispered.

For several seconds he gazed up at her in chilling expressionlessness, then he removed his hands from behind his head and held out his arms to her, the unexpectedness of his sudden smile bringing a lump to her throat.

'The first time can be so important,' he murmured as he drew her down into his arms. 'I'd never have forgiven myself if my impatience had frightened you away.'

CHAPTER SEVEN

THERE was a time during the night in which Daniel's complaining laughter startled Jane into wakefulness.

'That's the second time I've nearly fallen out of this damned bed,' he chuckled as he swept her up in his arms and began carrying her towards his own room.

It was some considerable time before they actually reached their destination and when they did his only words were a softly protesting, 'Have you any idea of what you do to me?' before passion engulfed them entirely.

She awoke the following morning to find him gazing down at her from remote and brooding eyes, his face shadowed with beard. Then he smiled, a tentative smile of such guileless sweetness that it sent scuttling into temporary oblivion all the doubts, all those yet-to-be-faced questions lurking sinister and unformed in her mind.

'How quickly your beard grows,' she whispered, her fingers reaching up to explore.

'That's because I didn't get around to shaving yesterday,' he replied, his words slightly constrained, yet his actions oddly affectionate as he began grazing his chin back and forth against her outstretched hand.

For several moments they remained silent, her hand against his face.

'I suppose, under the circumstances, you could hardly have just come out with it. . .and told me you were a virgin,' he stated quietly.

'I suppose not,' she agreed, her hand and his face

still maintaining their strangely affectionate link despite the stilted distancing of their words.

'I was thinking, he began, the hesitancy in his words stilling the breath in her. 'We could go shopping, if you like, and see what we could find for brunch... . I'm starving.'

The air trapped in her lungs expelled itself in laughter that was part relief, part disappointment. . .whatever she might have hoped or feared, those words had touched on neither.

'Are you sure you could last through a bout of shopping—being that hungry?'

'I'm sure,' he replied. 'You see, it isn't my appetite for food that's the problem—though if you don't remove yourself from my bed this instant there's a strong possibility I'll end up dead from hunger.' He lowered his head and kissed her briefly on the mouth. 'Be off with you, before my life becomes endangered,' he ordered, suddenly rolling her to the edge of the bed and tipping her on to the floor.

'I think I'd better cook Flynn's porridge,' she chuckled contentedly, picking herself up from the floor. 'We can't have you spoiling your appetite.'

She was happy, she told herself dreamily as she stepped from the shower and began dressing. It was an insecure happiness, beleaguered by uncertainties she had yet to find the will to face, yet greater than any she had ever experienced before.

Yet even as she finished dressing there was a voice of foreboding within her, warning her that last night had been no more than the beginning of an inevitable end; that he had always made it brutally clear that the day would come when she would have no option but to leave. . .when his ardour for her was finally spent. But there was another part of her that remembered Lyn's words about playing the odds, however slight; if any love stood a chance of begetting love, surely it was one as powerful as hers?

'I'm looking for Flynn's lead,' Daniel called to her as she entered the kitchen, his head inside one of the food cupboards.

'You won't find it there—it's in the utility-room,' she told him, her heart somersaulting wildly just at the sight of him.

He got the lead and appeared to be examining it minutely as he walked straight past her and out of the kitchen without so much as glancing in her direction.

'Flynn, Jane—get a move on, will you?' he called impatiently from the hall.

'You notice how it's you first and me a poor second,' she murmured to the dog, a feeling of sick apprehension seeping through her as she heard the naked bitterness that had crept into her words.

He was waiting by the car when the two of them caught up with him.

'As I suspected—you look good enough to eat,' he observed in a curiously flat tone of voice that brought wary uncertainty to her eyes. 'I didn't trust myself to look while we were inside,' he teased, catching her expression, 'for fear I wouldn't be able to keep my hands off you.'

He had feared he wouldn't be able to keep his hands off one of the new typists not so long ago, a censorious part of her sharply reminded her, but her heart had already returned to somersaulting dizzyingly, and a smile had leapt to her lips as she gazed up at him.

'You'd better drive,' he grinned, chucking her the car keys and vaulting into the passenger-seat as Flynn installed himself in the rear bucket-seat.

'What, me—drive this?' she protested in alarm.

'Why not? It's no different from any other car,' he retorted. 'In fact, it's a darn sight better than most.'

'Why can't you drive? What if I wreck it?'

'How can I possibly drive in my condition?' he demanded, as though she had suddenly lost her reason. 'And I shall be most annoyed if you wreck it.'

'What do you mean—your condition?' she exclaimed, then blushed to the roots as he gave her the most suggestive look she had ever received.

'Daniel Blake, you're——'

'Worn out, to put it rather delicately,' he cut in innocently. 'And perhaps the most intelligent thing to do would be to take a taxi, as you're probably almost as——'

'I'll drive,' she announced with a slightly breathless laugh, then climbed in beside him. 'No, let *me* do that,' she protested, her eyes twinkling, as he began fastening his seatbelt. 'We can't have you over-taxing yourself, now, can we?'

He dropped his chin to her head with a soft chuckle as she leaned across him.

'Tell me, is this touching concern of yours an indication that you have something particularly strenuous in store for me later?' he murmured, laughter rumbling lazily from him as the colour once more flew to her cheeks.

'You're quite some cook,' he told her later that evening from his vantage point at the kitchen table as he watched her prepare supper. 'Who taught you?'

'Nobody really, though I suppose I picked up a lot from Ted, my stepfather—he loves cooking,' she replied, part of her standing aside and attempting to gauge the picture they presented—the man seated at the table with his dog at his feet, a newspaper open

before him, from which he was reading sporadically. . .and the little woman tending to the supper,
she rounded off acerbically. But things certainly
weren't as they might appear. There was that almost
tangible atmosphere of constraint between them—as
though both felt driven to be on their best behaviour.
No, she corrected herself with a *frisson* of discomfort,
as though *he* felt driven and she felt obliged to follow.

Yet there had been the odd time during the day
when he had almost begun to relax, but each time it
had been as though an invisible rein had been
tugged, to which he had immediately responded. It
was only during their lovemaking that he had been
completely unrestrained.

She glanced over at him as she finished preparing
the salad dressing, her cheeks colouring as her senses
began throbbing with the memory of their return
from their morning's shopping. Was it always as
intense as this at the start of an affair, she wondered,
or was their insatiable need for each other something
out of the ordinary?

'Do you miss your stepsister—or weren't the two
of you that close?' he asked, catching her off guard
with the complete unexpectedness of the question.

'We're very close—and yes, I do miss her a lot.'
There were questions she wanted to ask him and it
disturbed her that something held her back from
coming straight out with them as he had just now.
'Do you have any stepbrothers or sisters?' she asked,
annoyed to hear a slight note of hesitancy in her
voice.

'Not that I know of,' he muttered, returning his
attention to the newspaper.

Jane's eyes rolled in disbelief as she turned to
check the cutlets under the grill, then she pulled
herself up sharply—she had asked a perfectly

straightforward question and had been palmed off
with a particularly crass answer.

'Daniel, don't be daft—of course you must know!'
she exclaimed with mild exasperation.

'OK—no, I haven't any stepbrothers or sisters.'

'So why say you didn't know?' she persisted,
goaded by the edge in his tone.

'Why the sudden third degree, Jane?' he enquired,
his head not rising from the newspaper.

It was his almost ritualistic calmness and politeness, when it was perfectly clear he was rattled, that
snapped something in her.

'In other words, the fact that I happen to have
shared your bed doesn't give me the right to ask
personal questions, is that it?'

'No—it isn't that at all,' he replied, after a lengthy
pause she had found decidedly nerve-racking. 'And
I apologise if that was the impression I gave.'

Totally perplexed, Jane gave a small shake of her
head. 'I'm sorry. . . I. . . Daniel, I really don't know
what made me come out with that,' she stammered,
hating herself for her dithering confusion and him
for causing it. Why couldn't he have just come and
put his arms round her instead of trotting out that
stiltedly formal apology?

'Jane, I'm the one to blame, not you,' he told her
quietly. 'It's just that my childhood was a little
confusing, to say the least—especially my parents'
predilection for multiple marriages. . .so it's something I'm not used to discussing.'

And something he had no intention of getting used
to discussing, she realised, and found herself oddly
disturbed at the thought of what a psychologist might
have to say on the matter.

'Would you like me to lay the table?' he offered,
the subject plainly closed as far as he was concerned.

Jane nodded, amusement flickering over her face.

'Do you intend sharing the joke?' he asked as he rose, the words pleasant enough, but his eyes slightly wary.

'I was just thinking that, apart from making tea and coffee, that's about all you're capable of in the kitchen.'

'Are you sure you intended wording it quite like that?' he asked, his eyes now teasing. 'Because I might just take you up on that—after we've eaten.' He chuckled softly as she made a big show of checking the food. 'And as for cooking—there's never been any need for me to do it for myself.'

Jane dished up the food, a vicious little demon of jealousy gnawing away at her as she effortlessly conjured up vivid images of a whole stream of her predecessors doing exactly what she was doing now.

'Well, perhaps it's about time you learned,' she said, the bright smile she gave him as she handed him a plate an attempt to take the sting out of the words.

'Why should I—when you're so great at it?' he murmured unconcernedly.

It was the most opportune of moments for her to point out that such a skill might come in useful after she had gone and to bring out into the open what was never far from her mind. . .but it was an opportunity she found herself unable to risk taking for fear of what his reply might be.

'Does my reluctance to talk about my childhood disturb you, Jane?' he asked as they began eating.

'No,' she lied.

'Good, because I'd hate to think it indicates I'm in need of mothering—or anything equally nauseating.'

'Is that a problem you have with women?' she asked sarcastically. 'That they all want to mother you?'

'What makes you think I have any problems with

women?' he drawled, helping himself to salad and surreptitiously passing Flynn a wedge of tomato.

Jane was about to treat him to her most withering look, but she suddenly thought better of it when it occurred to her that his cloak of painstaking politeness had just slipped.

'I thought you didn't approve of Flynn being fed at the table,' she accused instead.

He bowed his head in a parody of repentance.

'I don't—it's just that he loves tomatoes and he's been making eyes at me ever since we sat down,' he muttered sheepishly.

She gazed at him in exasperated amusement as he resumed eating, a question springing to her mind that she hesitated over before asking.

'Daniel, why did you only ever have one dog before Flynn?'

The instant she saw the wariness in his eyes, she knew it was the thought of his clamming up once more that had made her hesitate.

'My mother's maternal instincts used to flare up on the odd occasion, and it was during one such spell that I was bundled off to her in Scotland where she happened to be at the time. She wouldn't hear of my bringing the dog up with me; when I returned home he had gone.'

'How do you mean—gone?'

'Just gone. He wasn't particularly well-trained and someone must have left the gates open.'

'And you never saw him again?' asked Jane in consternation.

'I spent months roaming London looking for him——'

'What age were you?' she gasped.

'Around nine or ten—and no, I never did find him.'

Jane had a vivid mental picture of the two boys,

Mark and Jonathan, heartbroken as they scoured the streets, and suddenly she felt very cold.

'But you obviously love dogs,' she protested sadly. 'What made you leave it until now before getting another?'

He shrugged. 'Having cut my emotional losses that young, later it never really occurred to me to have another. I got Flynn by default—a friend had ordered a dog but got a sudden posting abroad.'

'So Flynn actually lived with someone else first?'

'No—he came to me straight from the kennels. He's a very well-bred lad, you know; I believe he's got a pedigree as long as your arm—not that that sort of thing matters in the least to me.'

'Was your other dog a retriever?'

He shook his head, but he made no mention of what breed his other dog had been. And Jane found herself wondering just how many times he had been obliged to cut his emotional losses as a child. . .and what sort of effect it had had on the man.

'It's unlikely to be for me,' he said, as the telephone suddenly rang. 'I'm supposed to be in France—remember?' he added with a grin as Jane got to her feet.

She unhooked the receiver from the wall and heard a woman's voice in response to hers—not Lyn's as she had wondered if it might be, but a melodious, though plainly slightly startled voice, asking to speak to Daniel.

He rose with reluctance to take the receiver she held out to him, the chilly remoteness she had come to recognise settling on his handsome features as he announced himself and then listened.

'Hello, Katrina,' he said, pausing once more to listen. 'No, I shan't be. . . I really didn't see any necessity. . .no, of course it had nothing to do with that.' There followed another, longer pause. 'I'm sure

I don't know where you got that idea, but certainly not from anything I might have said. . .no, not really, if you don't mind. . .no. Goodbye.' He replaced the receiver, an expression of mild irritation on his face. 'It's odd, isn't it, that, no matter how unequivocally certain statements may be worded, there are always those who manage to misinterpret them?' he muttered half to himself, while Jane hurriedly disengaged herself from her attempts to fill in the missing sections of the conversation as he returned to the table.

'Would you like some fruit?' she asked when they had finished eating, unsettled to find herself having to keep dragging her mind away from the missing half of that overheard conversation.

He shook his head. 'No, thanks, but I'll make some coffee—later,' he offered, suddenly leaning across the table and kissing the tip of her nose. 'Thanks for a delicious meal,' he murmured, as Jane did battle with the overwhelming surge of love awoken in her by that careless gesture of tenderness.

'Just you make sure the coffee lives up to it,' she joked to hide her confusion as it suddenly occurred to her that that light-hearted kiss was the only demonstration of affection he had displayed to her all day that hadn't been overtly sexual.

'Actually, the coffee's only the third item on the agenda,' he informed her with a chuckle, rising and beginning to stack the dishes. 'First we clear this lot away.'

'And second?'

'We haven't finished the first yet,' he parried.

'We? I cooked!' she protested in mock indignation. 'But I'm making the coffee!'

'How can you possibly equate cooking an entire meal with producing a pot of coffee?' she exclaimed

through laughter—then gave in and began helping
him as he proceeded to attempt precisely that.

When they had finished, he held out a hand to
her, grinning. 'Second, we get our sleeping arrangements sorted out,' he announced, disregarding her
decidedly startled expression as he hauled her by the
hand, out of the kitchen and up the stairs.

He marched her down the corridor to their left.

'We can forget about those two over there,' he
muttered, jerking his head dismissively towards two
unused rooms across the huge galleried stairwell as
he dragged her along. 'How about this?' he
exclaimed, flinging open the door before them and
then, before she could even open her mouth to beg
an explanation, hauling her off to yet another room.
'Or this?' he demanded as he threw open the door.

Jane turned to him in total bewilderment.

'Daniel, it would help if I had just the tiniest idea
of what all this is about,' she protested weakly.

'We need a room the two of us can share, don't
we?' he asked with a touch of impatience. 'I thought
we might as well get the selection over and done
with.'

Jane's eyes dropped from his, an inexplicable feeling of unease prickling through her.

'After all, there are so many rooms in the house,
we ought to use them,' he stated, as though set on
convincing her. 'One for you, one for me, and one
for us, so to speak.'

'Oh,' managed Jane, trying desperately to shrug
off her totally illogical unease.

'Oh?' he queried, releasing her hand. 'You don't
think it's such a good idea,' he stated quietly.

She hesitated fractionally—there was nothing she
could honestly find fault with it, she reasoned
reluctantly.

'I think it's a very good idea,' she found herself

saying. 'I was just puzzled as to why you rejected the other two rooms out of hand.'

'Because one has twin beds and the other a single,' he replied wryly, placing a hand on her shoulder and turning her to face him fully. 'But there's something about my suggestion you're not happy with,' he added quietly.

'It's not that I'm not happy with it,' she muttered miserably. 'I. . . I suppose it was something I just hadn't thought about in any detail.'

'Jane, I. . .the truth is, I've never actually lived with a woman before. . . I've probably gone about this all wrong.'

He had sensed that he had upset her and, though he was unable to understand why any more than she was, this tentative, somewhat oblique apology was his attempt to make amends, she realised, and was suddenly very touched.

'Well, if you're worried about not knowing the rules, there's always me for you to consult,' she told him softly, her face completely straight. 'After all, I've lived with dozens of men.'

Even before she had all the words out, he had swept her off her feet in a suffocating bear hug.

'I think you'd better pin up a list of those rules somewhere prominent,' he told her huskily, 'because I've a feeling we're going to need them rather frequently.' He returned her to her feet. 'So. . .where do we go from here?'

'I suppose we decide on a room,' she replied breathlessly, her vague doubts thoroughly dispelled.

'*We*?' he exclaimed, his eyes twinkling. 'I suggest *you* get on with making the choice, while I rustle up some bed-linen—in case you've forgotten, *I* still have the coffee to make after we've finished all this!'

CHAPTER EIGHT

'SORRY to barge in like this, but could you spare a minute?' Without waiting for a reply, Joan Sellers closed the door of Jane's office behind her and walked straight to the desk. 'It's just that I'll go mad if I can't let off steam to. . .well, to someone who's probably in the same boat,' gushed Joan, flinging herself down on the chair before the desk.

'I beg your pardon?' croaked Jane and was immediately cross with herself for giving away how completely thrown she was by this unexpected intrusion.

'It's just that Katrina arrived back on Monday evening and——' Joan broke off with a totally uncharacteristically skittish laugh. 'Oh, dear, I suppose I really should explain before leaping in like that!' she exclaimed, her repeated laugh grating on Jane's ears. 'It's just that I've known from the word go about Daniel's grandmother's will and everything,' she continued breathily. 'I mean, it was only natural that Daniel would have to explain it all to Katrina—especially as a strange woman was about to move into his house!' This time her laugh implied she found the whole idea hilarious. 'I suppose you can hardly blame Katrina for kicking up the stink she did. . . In the end, Daniel had no choice but to bundle her off to France, practically by force, in order to try to make her see sense.'

'Joan, is there any particular reason for your telling me all this?' asked Jane quietly, knowing full well that, whatever the reason, it wasn't likely to bode her any good.

'Not really,' sighed Joan, flashing her a look of

girlish complicity which had Jane almost squirming in her seat with its blatant insincerity. 'It's just that there comes a time when it helps to be able to let off a bit of steam to someone who understands.'

'Well, I'm afraid I *don't* understand,' stated Jane firmly, praying Lyn would return soon and have the wit to ring through and find out if she needed rescuing. 'To be frank, I haven't the slightest idea what you're talking about.'

'I suppose it's only natural that Daniel would hide his feelings better than Katrina does,' sighed Joan, undeterred. 'But you can bet your bottom dollar he's hurting every bit as much as she is inside. People in love can behave so ludicrously at times——'

'Joan, look, I'm sorry, but whatever it is you have to say, I really don't think I'm the person for you to be saying it to,' interrupted Jane, angry with herself to find those last words twisting in her like a knife.

'I suppose I am being a bit of a pain!' exclaimed Joan with no trace of contrition in her tone. 'But you can't imagine what it's been like since those two fell in love. That's not to say that it hasn't been lovely and romantic—because they're obviously made for each other—but they say the course of true love never runs smoothly. I keep telling Katrina it's hardly Daniel's fault his wretched grandmother left you half his house.' The words babbled out of her with no chance for Jane to interrupt without resorting to shouting her down. 'And, heaven knows, Daniel's tried his best to make her understand nothing's changed. I thought it was so sweet of him to take her off to his place in Juan-les-Pins—they've more or less decided on having their wedding there next year— so why on earth she should feel the need to make him so jealous by flirting with——'

'Joan, as I've already said, I'm not the person you should be discussing this with,' snapped Jane, rising to her feet, then diving for the suddenly ringing telephone as though for a lifeline.

'Thanks Lyn. . .' she cut through her assistant's tentative query as to whether she needed any help '. . . I'll be right out to have a look at it.'

Joan Sellers rose to her feet, the cloying mask of friendliness slipping from her face. 'I'm sorry—I'd no idea my innocent quest for a sympathetic shoulder would upset you so much,' she stated, a familiar sneer now in her tone.

'I'd be most surprised to discover there was anything you'd ever done innocently,' blurted out Jane, and was immediately angry for allowing herself to become reduced to this unpleasant woman's level.

'My, my, I really do seem to have hit on a raw nerve, don't I?' crowed Joan as she moved towards the door. 'I don't blame you for trying to land him yourself—he's a very attractive and, of course, extremely wealthy man.' She gave a mocking laugh as she opened the door. 'Unfortunately for you, he's also well and truly spoken for. . .and there's nothing whatsoever you can do about it.'

'So, what was all that about?' demanded Lyn, striding determinedly towards Jane as the outer office door slammed shut.

'To be honest, I'm not really sure,' muttered Jane dazedly, her scattered thoughts trying to make some sense of those past few bewildering moments and getting nowhere.

'Jane, you're as white as a sheet!' exclaimed Lyn angrily. 'Whatever that ghastly creature had to say, I'd have thought you, of all people, would have the sense to take no notice of it!'

'I didn't,' protested Jane confusedly. 'I. . . Lyn, it's just that I can't for the life of me understand what prompted her to come out with what she did.'

'Well, you can bet your sweet life she has her

reasons,' muttered Lyn darkly, walking round the desk and perching herself on its top right beside Jane, 'and all of them thoroughly unpleasant.'

Jane gazed up at her and nodded. 'Just give me a moment to collect my wits,' she pleaded, closing her eyes.

'Jane, you don't have to tell me if you don't want to——'

'Of course I want to tell you,' protested Jane, her eyes flying open in consternation. 'In fact, there's something else I've been trying to psych myself up into telling you for the past few days,' she admitted nervously.

'That you and Danny Boy are lovers?' asked Lyn gently.

Jane's heart plummeted. 'I'm that transparent, am I?' she muttered dejectedly.

'Jane, I know you too well—I spot differences in you that others never would,' pointed out Lyn in that same gently caring voice. 'I think I knew the instant he brought you to work—I mean, right up to your office—on Monday morning. But if either of you was transparent, it was Danny Boy.'

'Lyn, it isn't the way it might seem,' protested Jane wearily. The main reason she hadn't been able to bring herself to tell Lyn was that she knew her friend would automatically leap to all the wrong conclusions. . .though what the right conclusions were she had no idea.

'Let me tell you how it seems to me—just the plain, unadorned facts as I see them—and then you tell me what I'm seeing wrong,' stated Lyn, eyeing her candidly. 'Danny Boy comes haring back here to settle some business—right? It appears he still regards himself as on holiday because so far this week he's only drifted into the office now and then for the odd hour or so. Any objections so far?'

Jane shook her head, gazing down at her hands clenched tightly in her lap.

'Yet he hasn't gone back to resume his holiday in France, as one would have expected. Instead he's taken to chauffeuring you back and forth to work. . .making a special journey to fetch you each evening.'

'Lyn, you're reading far too much into that,' protested Jane, something she had been warning herself against doing with monotonous regularity all week.

'Jane, Danny Boy's not stupid; whether people know about his grandmother's will is immaterial—he knows perfectly well they're all bound to sit up and take notice when the boss starts playing chauffeur to one of his staff. . . Oh, heck!' she suddenly exclaimed. 'That creature's visit hadn't by any chance anything to do with her cousin—what's her name——?'

'Katrina——'

'The one he's obviously abandoned in France! Oh, Jane, you idiot!'

'Lyn, just let me tell you what she said,' pleaded Jane and immediately launched into it before she could be interrupted.

'Talk about hell having no fury like a cousin of Joan Sellers scorned,' chortled Lyn when Jane had finished. 'For heaven's sake, Jane, how could you have let drivel like that upset you?' she demanded indignantly.

'Why drivel?' asked Jane quietly. 'He took Katrina to France——'

'And nearly broke his neck in his rush back to her?'

'Lyn, please. . .you don't understand. Twisting the truth seems to come as easily to Joan as breathing—heaven knows, I've had to deal with the repercussions of it often enough among those who had to work with her—but even you have to admit she's not stupid, and she knows all I have to do is check her story with Daniel to find out if she's lying or not.'

'But are you sure that isn't something she's banking on your not doing?' asked Lyn quietly. 'And, anyway, can you imagine Danny Boy kicking his heels around here with the alleged love of his life still in France?'

'I don't know!' exclaimed Jane, horrified to find herself close to tears. 'And I don't really care. . .all I know is that I can't go on like this much longer!' She gave a brittle little laugh of disbelief. 'I'd already decided to swallow my pride and cut my losses. . .why did he have to come back?'

Lyn slid off the table-top and balanced herself on the arm of Jane's chair, hugging her protectively.

'Jane, is there something you haven't told me?' she demanded anxiously.

'No. . . I. . . Lyn, I can't even explain it to myself, so how can I possibly expect to explain it to you?' she sighed, furiously blinking back the tears.

Without actually coming right out and saying it, she knew she was fighting a losing battle in trying to describe the contrast between the passionately un-inihibited man who was her lover and that other, studiously polite, almost remote man that he was the rest of the time. . .but she tried.

'You obviously must have some theories on why he should be behaving like this,' observed Lyn when those haltingly garbled words finally petered to silence.

'I suppose guilt is the most common cause of people's feeling ill at ease,' replied Jane tonelessly.

'Guilt over what?'

Jane shrugged. 'Perhaps leaving Katrina and starting an affair with me. . .in a fit of jealousy.'

'Surely you can come up with something a bit more convincing than that?' exclaimed Lyn exasperatedly.

'You even managed to sound as though you knew you were talking a load of rubbish!'

Probably because she was pretty certain she had been, Jane conceded wearily to herself. Unless Daniel was one of the finest actors around, he hadn't appeared in the least upset by Katrina's call—irritated, yes, but certainly not like a man thwarted in love.

'Damn!' exclaimed Lyn as the telephone in her office began ringing. 'I'll be back in a tick.'

As Jane watched Lyn dash out of the door, it was almost as though she felt something click into place in her mind. Guilt, she suddenly realised, was not quite the right word for the unease that often seemed to exude from Daniel; embarrassment now struck her as far more apt a word. The embarrassment of a man regretting having uttered words which could never be retracted.

He had been right in his coldly confident prediction that they would become lovers. And now, for whatever reason—perhaps no more than an intrinsic decency—he regretted having spelled out in coldness how that affair must inevitably end. And now he must be realising how much easier it would have been had he remained silent and just let their inevitable affair run its inevitable course.

Inevitable—how she hated that word! Why couldn't it have been as inevitable for him to love her as it had been for her to love him?

'Sorry about that; it was John,' apologised Lyn, reappearing in the doorway. 'He was telling me. . . Flynn! How are you, boy?' she exclaimed delightedly, her delight turning to rueful laughter as the dog bounded straight past her and over to Jane.

'It's disgusting, isn't it?' came Daniel's amused voice from behind her. 'He even tramples me underfoot to get to her—and I'm supposed to be his master!'

Jane glanced across at the man and the girl in the doorway, acutely conscious of the warm colour creeping over her cheeks as she petted Flynn.

'Don't you believe it,' she smiled.

'Did you hear that? She's just called me a liar!' exclaimed Daniel indignantly, winking at Lyn who promptly patted him sympathetically on the arm.

He was so relaxed with Lyn, thought Jane with pangs of sadness and envy. . .so relaxed, in fact, that Lyn could easily be forgiven for regarding anyone describing him as ill at ease as being in need of psychiatric help.

'Now, I realise it isn't even half-past four yet,' Daniel was saying to Lyn, 'but is there any chance of my whisking Jane away early. . .just this once?'

'Well,' pondered Lyn, pursing her lips and frowning deeply, 'I'd need your word that this isn't going to develop into a habit.'

'You have my solemn oath,' he vowed, clutching vaguely at his chest.

'The heart's usually situated on the left,' cued Lyn from the corner of her mouth.

He obligingly clutched the other side.

'Well, I'm still not convinced,' stalled Lyn, then leapt aside with a giggled shriek as he switched tactics and began threatening her with a clenched fist.

'I think we'd better make a dash for it before she decides to call Security,' he called to Jane as Lyn ducked under his arm to answer a ringing telephone.

Jane grabbed her bag and joined him, her expression one of puzzled amusement.

'Actually, we'd better get a move on,' he said, catching her by the arm and giving Lyn a hurried wave goodbye. 'I've parked in the street. . .usually a traffic warden shows up before I have the keys out of the ignition.'

They raced out of the building and dived into the car under the disapproving nose of a traffic warden, Flynn at their heels. And as they sped off Daniel turned and gave her a smile that started up such a torrent of love in her that she felt almost in danger of drowning in it.

'Jane, I'm not in the least sure how you're going to react to hearing the reason for my dashing round and collecting you in such a rush,' he admitted, flashing her another of those smiles.

'I thought you just happened to be in the vicinity,' she replied, her gaze questioning.

'I came across some of my grandmother's diaries the other day—I'd forgotten what an avid diary-keeper she was.' His glance flickered towards her, then away. 'Anyway, it started me wondering if there were any more of them around. . .and today I found them in one of the attics.'

'And then you came round to collect me,' stated Jane, a peculiarly hollow feeling settling in the pit of her stomach.

He nodded, the look he gave her pensive and slightly guarded.

'Did you find anything of interest in them?' she asked, struggling to keep her tone light.

'I didn't read them. Well, I flicked one open at random. . .to be honest, it spooked me slightly— reading it—so I closed it.'

Jane said nothing as he swung the car into the drive, but she was conscious of him following her as she leapt out and went to close the gates.

'Perhaps it wasn't such a good idea,' he muttered, helping her with the gates, 'coming to get you on the spur of the moment like that. Perhaps I should have thought twice about even mentioning them to you.'

Jane shook her head vigorously. 'I just didn't think it would affect me like this. . .the idea of perhaps being able to find out what I've always wanted to know.'

' "Perhaps" being the operative word,' he warned her, slipping an arm lightly across her shoulders as they walked towards the house. 'There's always the chance they won't tell us anything we can make sense of.' His arm dropped from around her as he opened the door, but he caught her by the shoulder as they entered, turning her towards him. 'It's just that when we spoke of what had happened between our families I sensed a need in you to know exactly what it all had been about. . .though if the idea upsets you I can return the relevant diaries to the loft,' he told her quietly.

She shook her head, his words making her feel almost as though he had read her mind and seen the doubts scurrying around inside her, pulling her in opposite directions.

'There was a time. . .so many years, when the need to know was like a desperation. Yet now I'm almost frightened by the thought of what I might learn. . .but I couldn't possibly not read them. . .could I?'

'Perhaps you should have a think about it,' he suggested. 'Why don't you go and get changed and I'll make some tea?'

'No—I think I'd like to get it over and done with now,' she stated, the words grating like sandpaper against her tongue.

He led her into one of the sitting-rooms.

'Would you like a drink?' he asked, pouring himself a whisky.

'No—thanks. Where are they?'

He went to the bureau, then returned with a large diary, much larger than Jane had envisaged, with the name Dorothy Blake and the year stamped in fine gold leaf on its dark green leather binding.

'This is the relevant year,' he said, handing it to her. 'I also brought down the year before and a couple after—just in case you needed to refer to them.'

Jane sat down on the large sofa, the diary resting in her hand like a lead weight.

Daniel sat down beside her, pulling her down against his shoulder as he placed an arm around her and took the diary from her.

'From what I remember, Joe and Robert had parted company by October,' he said. 'Perhaps if we go back to around May or June we'll start finding clues—if there are any.'

Holding the book before them so that they could both read it, he began leafing through page after dense page of perfectly executed copper-plate writing.

It had been on a Thursday in the second week in July, they discovered, that Dolly had learned of her husband's taunting disclosure to his partner of his duplicity of so long ago.

'I don't think I'd have liked to get on the wrong side of your grandmother,' gasped Jane, as the dead woman's fury with both men leapt out at them from the pages.

'And you'd have been right not to,' agreed Daniel. 'But do you notice how, even then, she never let Robert know it was her love of him that had led her to ditching Joe like that?'

Jane nodded, feeling almost nauseous with the tension now gripping her and suddenly realising how strangely oblivious her body was to the enveloping closeness of his.

'Daniel. . .would you mind skimming through it and reading out the relevant bits?' she asked as the words suddenly began to dance drunkenly before her eyes.

'How am I to know what's relevant?' he muttered, even as he began doing as she had asked. 'What was your grandmother's name?' he demanded suddenly.

'Jessica—why?' she croaked, the blood seeming to freeze in her veins.

'It seems they were quite close—Dolly and Jessica,' he muttered, continuing to read.

'What does it say about her? Is she sick by this time?'

'Hang on. Heavens—no wonder Dolly was in such a rage with both men!' he exclaimed, turning over a page and continuing to read.

For several minutes he read on, saying nothing.

'It's something horrible, isn't it?' she asked distractedly, burying her face against him.

'It's beginning to make some sense,' he replied, his words making no attempt to answer her anguished question. 'Jane, would you rather read it yourself?' he asked gently.

She shook her head, pressing her face deeper against him.

'You'd rather I just read on until I start getting the whole picture?'

She nodded, fully aware that she was probably making a spectacle of herself, but unable to do anything about it. She raised her head slightly when she felt his chin nuzzle against her hair.

'Jane, you've got to try keeping it in mind that none of this can alter anything now. . .it's all dead and buried in the past,' he told her quietly.

'I know that,' she sighed. . .but knowing it couldn't alter what was taking place inside her, she thought agitatedly. If ever she had children, she silently vowed, there would be no family skeleton, however terrible, however trivial, that she would ever keep from them. Her own childhood, she now faced, had been blighted by half-truths and ignorance. . .neither her father nor her mother, who had both loved her, had ever recognised the terrible yearning in her to know what had driven him to leave them. 'You've finished?' she whispered, a suffocating stillness entering her as he put down the diary.

'Enough to have a pretty good idea of what happened,' he replied, his arm tightening around her. 'How it affected your father is what you really want to know, isn't it, Jane?'

She nodded, feeling that the terrible tension in her was the only thing holding her together.

'All I can do is put two and two together and make an educated guess,' he warned her.

'I realise that,' she replied, suddenly glad of the warmth of him next to her and the support of his arm around her.

'Jessica died of tetanus. It's apparently something difficult to diagnose unless it's being looked for specifically, and in her case it was detected too late for her to be saved.'

'I don't remember anyone ever mentioning what she died of,' said Jane, part of her searching for words to stall his while another part of her silently cried out for him to continue.

'Jane, everything points to your father's having had a complete mental breakdown—and no wonder, given the appalling mental burdens heaped on him in so short a space of time.' He lowered his chin to her head, rubbing it gently back and forth as he seemed to search for words. 'There were two major factors that combined to tip him over the edge. The first being that, however irrational, he held himself responsible for his mother's death. It seems that she was a keen gardener, unlike your parents, and that she had decided to do something about the mess she considered their garden to be. One day she cut her hand while doing the garden—your father actually helped dress the wound—and it was that cut which eventually led to her death. He maintained that had he thought to mention it to the doctors puzzling over her symptoms weeks later her life would have been saved.'

'He couldn't possibly have known its significance!' protested Jane, a lump catching in her throat.

'Of course he couldn't,' agreed Daniel. 'But now we come to the second and, perhaps, most crucial factor. Jessica was already a pretty sick woman, though no one yet realised it, the day Joe and my grandfather had that fateful row. Apparently they'd row anywhere and everywhere at the drop of a hat—this particular one took place in Joe's garden.' He hesitated, clearing his throat before continuing. 'Your father had just dropped by to see how his mother was and heard the whole slanging match from the driveway. It was only when he entered the house that he realised his mother had also heard every word of it from where she was resting in the conservatory.'

'Oh, no!' groaned Jane, her imagination conjuring up sickeningly vivid pictures. 'How on earth must the poor woman have felt?'

Daniel reached over for his whisky glass and took a sip from it.

'That's where it all starts getting complicated,' he told her. 'According to Dolly—and you have to remember that she and Jessica were quite close—Jessica was simply enraged that two grown men could behave so ridiculously. You have to remember that both women had had to contend with similar outbursts with monotonous regularity over the years, though this one seems to have topped the lot.'

'It could hardly have been pleasant for my grand-mother—hearing her husband ranting over his loss of another woman all those years ago!' exclaimed Jane bitterly.

'I think it might help to read what Dolly has to say about it all. She maintains that Jessica was always totally confident that Joe loved her deeply, and that she had every right to be. She also maintains—because Jessica actually told her—that it was in a fit of temper, on hearing them rowing when she felt so under the weather, that made Jessica announce she had had enough and was leaving Joe.' He reached down and took one of her hands, interlocking his fingers with hers. 'But what your father saw—and which nothing anyone later said could dissuade him from believing—was his mother devastated by the discovery that she had been second best where her husband's love was concerned. As her condition deteriorated and she was taken into hospital, he watched his mother die, convinced that her heart was broken.'

The feelings those words aroused in Jane sliced through her like wounding knives until her fingers squeezed frantically on his as she fought the temptation to cover her ears and blot out their sounds.

'Whichever way the poor devil turned, there was no peace to be found. He blamed himself for her condition's not being diagnosed in time. . .and he blamed his father for the broken heart he was con-vinced nothing could have cured.'

When the tears started choking from her, Daniel placed both his arms around her and began rocking her gently back and forth.

'If only someone had *told* me. . .just told me the facts!' she sobbed. 'Oh, my poor father, my poor, tortured father!'

'Jane, it won't always hurt this badly,' he tried to

comfort her. 'And, terrible though it all was, both your father and mother managed to come through it in the end.'

She tore herself from his arms, a sick, helpless rage possessing her.

'How can you say that? Their life together—all the love they had for one another—was destroyed! My only contact with him were letters—he was my father!'

'Jane, please——'

'I never saw him again. . .all I had were letters he sent me from Brazil. . . Brazil! Neither he nor my mother could bring themselves to mention what had happened to me, because silence was the glue holding together their survival.'

'Jane, why don't we just leave this for now—go out and have a meal somewhere——?'

'A meal? Eat?' she screamed at him. 'Only a Blake could think of his stomach at a time like this! If it hadn't been for your grandfather none of this would have happened. . .my father would probably still have been alive today!'

CHAPTER NINE

IT WAS long after Jane had cried herself into a stupor of exhaustion that awareness began seeping slowly back into her. It was the sensation of being alone that first struck her, and it grew till she was filled with an edgy, restless need. She had returned automatically to the room that had been hers alone and now both her body and mind were rejecting that action.

She rose from the bed and stumbled to the window, pressing her head against the cool of the glass. Tomorrow she would write to her mother, not to tell of what she had learned from the diaries, but to tell her of Dolly's will, she promised herself, and knew then that, although there would always be a part of her that grieved what fate had denied her parents, the savage immediacy of that grief was now purged from her.

She turned from the window, hugging her arms around herself in the pale coldness of the moonlight. And now there was loving Daniel to contend with and that disturbing blend of passion and constraint that constituted their life together. The conviction that she would one day lose him had become a repressed and silent terror lurking within her, so tainting her with its omnipresent threat that she had been unable to perceive the kindness and generosity of spirit that had governed his actions of this evening.

She felt a savage need grow in her simply for his presence: just to be able to hear the rhythmic softness of his breathing as he slept; just to have the warm masculine scent of him in her nostrils as her body lay next to his.

Just as she had fled to the solitude of her own room, so he would have returned to his, she told herself, her thoughts bitter and self-accusing as she slowly walked to the door and out into the corridor. Perhaps she would be able to bear the loneliness of this room no more than she had her own, she thought as she made her way towards the room they had chosen as theirs—but at least there was the chance that here she would feel that bit closer to him.

She closed the door behind her and walked to the bed, her heart swelling suffocatingly in her chest as she encountered the dark outline of his sleeping body.

He had detected the terrible need in her to know the facts of the past and had acted to assuage her need, a voice from within accused. Her reaction had been to hurl his kindness back in his face with a spiteful attack. . .yet it had been their room and not his own in which he now slept. . .almost as though he was waiting for her to come to him.

Disturbed to find her thoughts veering towards fantasy, she lifted the quilt and slipped under it beside him, a softly shivered sigh of love whispering from her as he turned and drew her into his arms.

'Daniel——'

'No—don't say anything,' he protested sleepily. 'Don't say anything.'

He held her in the silence of that strangely passive embrace until she could bear it no longer. Yet, when his body began responding to the fevered impatience of hers, it was in a way she found disconcertingly unfamiliar.

'No,' he whispered to her several times as their lovemaking threatened to deteriorate into a struggle by each for dominance over the other's needs.

It was a struggle his body eventually won, suddenly stilling the recklessness of passion in hers in a swift and impatient display of superior strength. And it was then she discovered that what he had been offering her was tenderness; something so deceptively sweet that the breathless suddenness of the sense-shattering eroticism it awoke in her brought soft cries of protest spilling from her. From tenderness through rapture he led her on, until their cries at last mingled in the wonderment of total fulfilment.

'Do you really *have* to go to work today?' he had pleaded with her the following morning, and the words had been almost like a declaration of love to her ears.

'Daniel Blake, you're not by any chance trying to lead one of your employees astray, are you?' she had teased, love almost dancing on her lips. 'Besides, Lyn's off on holiday next week and I couldn't possibly desert her with all we have to get sorted out before she goes.'

'But you've no qualms about deserting me,' he had growled, tipping her without warning out of the bed. 'So, if that's the way you feel,' he had added, grinning down wickedly at her, 'I suppose I've no choice but to follow your lousy example and put in a day's work myself.'

A dreamy smile of contentment drifted over her face as she wondered if he had got through as much work as she had. She doubted it. . .today she had floated through a mountain of work like someone possessed.

'We might as well tackle as much as we can,' Lyn had agreed that morning, her look teasing, 'because you're bound to be stretched way beyond your limits without me next week.'

She laughed softly to herself as she remembered Lyn's ragged comment of a few hours later.

'Jane, this holiday of mine is going to turn into a

period of convalescence if we keep this up—what's got into you?'

She had eased up on Lyn, but not on herself, she realised with a small stab of disquiet. By immersing herself so completely in her work she was allowing no room for her thoughts to go careering off on the flights of fantasy constantly beckoning them.

But would it necessarily be fantasy? Last night it had seemed like a certainty to her—that she was being loved, not simply being made love to. And this morning it had still been with her, that tremulous feeling of being bathed in love.

It was the fierce intensity of that uncorroborated certainty that increased her feelings of disquiet and made her respond almost with relief to the sudden ringing of the telephone on her desk.

'Miss Ashford—Jane Ashford?'

'Yes.'

'Polly Nestor here.'

Jane's eyes widened with surprise to hear the woman's brisk voice declare she was a reporter with a well-known, if not particularly highly thought of, newspaper.

'I was wondering if you would care to confirm a few facts with me regarding an article we might be doing on Blake Enterprises.'

Jane hesitated. The complete unexpectedness of such a call had thrown her; that it should have come from a newspaper she could scarcely believe even contained a financial section she found even more surprising.

'Are you really sure I'm the person who can help you?' she asked a little tentatively.

'Absolutely sure,' replied the woman. 'Your name was previously Jane Marley, wasn't it?'

Jane confirmed that it was, relaxing slightly as she

answered further questions establishing her relationship with one of the co-founders of the company.

'Do you feel that your experience as a personnel officer qualifies you to take over joint management of a business as complex as Blake Enterprises?'

'I'm sorry, but I find that a rather ridiculous question!' exclaimed Jane impatiently. 'If it's facts you want, I'm quite prepared to give you those I can, but——'

'Miss Ashford, by all accounts, the Blake-Marley family feud is still alive and kicking, thanks to you and Daniel Blake——'

'I'm sorry, I'm not answering questions as. . . as——'

'It's only by asking these questions that I can check how factual my information is,' pointed out the reporter blandly. 'Your refusal to sign your shares over to Daniel Blake——'

'I've no intention of signing my shares over to anyone!' exclaimed Jane exasperatedly. 'What I *have* signed over——'

'As I said, I'm just trying to check out the facts,' cut in that brisk, disembodied voice.

'Well, if you'd let me have my say, instead of interrupting all the time, perhaps you'd find the task that much easier,' retorted Jane, hardly able to credit the woman's nerve.

'OK, point taken,' came the unapologetic response. 'The fact that you're living with one of the most eligible bachelors around——'

'I'm living in the half of the house his grandmother left me,' corrected Jane wearily—this was unbelievable!

'Oh, so the house has been divided up, has it?'

'No, of course it hasn't!' snapped Jane, suddenly coming to her senses and realising she should have ended this ridiculous farce several minutes ago. 'I'm sorry, but I have work to attend to. Goodbye.' She slammed down the receiver and flew out to Lyn's office.

'How weird,' said Lyn, once the bizarre conversation had been related to her. 'That particular rag isn't exactly renowned for the accuracy of its reporting—but you seem to have put Polly Nestor firmly in her place,' she chuckled. 'So I'd just forget it if I were you.'

'I can hardly claim to have put her in her place,' pointed out Jane irritably. 'The wretched woman hardly let me get a word in.'

'Well I'm sure she got the general drift of your message,' soothed Lyn. 'So stop prowling around like a caged cat.'

Jane continued pacing, frowning as a thought suddenly occurred to her. 'Lyn, I know she got it wrong. . .but how did she know I'd refused to sign something in connection with my share-holding?'

Lyn shook her head in puzzlement. 'As you say, she got it wrong—so perhaps it was no more than a shot in the dark. They're so incredibly devious, those sorts of reporters—for instance, how did she get hold of the number of the direct line to your office?' She laughed suddenly. 'Come to think of it, she probably used up any investigative skills she may possess just finding that out!'

Jane chuckled, her bemused indignation dissipating. 'Well, she should have saved herself the trouble, because one thing's for sure: if she rings again I'm hanging up on her.'

'That's my girl,' teased Lyn, her eyes twinkling. 'And now back to the grindstone—what about those junior staff salary reviews?'

'What about them?' grinned Jane. 'I've finished the lot!'

* * *

'I wonder if Mark and Jonathan have their own Flynn yet,' said Daniel, as they strolled back from the park that evening.

'Don't worry, you'll be hearing the moment they have,' smiled Jane, a contentment such as none she had ever known before warming its way throughout her as they reached the house. 'I gave them your number. I met their mother the last time I saw them—she seemed so nice,' she added as she helped him close the gates.

'Yes—they seem an unusually happy family,' he remarked, picking up a stick lying in the drive and throwing it for Flynn.

Jane walked towards the house, listening to his groaned protests as Flynn kept retrieving the stick and begging for it to be thrown again, sadness diluting her happiness because Daniel automatically assumed a happy family to be an unusual one.

'No, Flynn, that's enough!' he protested, laughing. 'Go and pester Jane.'

'You can count Jane out,' she laughed, racing into the house. 'She has the supper to see to.'

Once or twice as she prepared the meal, and again later as they ate it, she wondered if now might be the moment to make the apology she had yet to offer him for her appalling outburst the night before. She had tried that morning, but he had deliberately distracted her and she had felt no option but to let the matter drop.

Later she found herself pondering over his deliberate distracting of her; whatever his reasons, he obviously hadn't wanted to discuss it this morning. It was hardly something they could pretend hadn't happened, she fretted uncertainly before deciding to leave it for now. Knowing Daniel as she did, the moment he felt like raising the subject he would do so without any hesitation.

'I'm sure if you ask her nicely Jane will take you out to play now,' he informed the dog lying contentedly at his feet.

'He's showing about as much enthusiasm as I feel about a romp in the rain and dark,' laughed Jane, dragging her gaze away from his handsome, teasing face and watching the rain lashing noisily against the windows. Now was one of those times when she could hardly bear to look at him for fear of the love that her eyes must betray. She had spent the entire journey home from work with her eyes secretly loving him as he had concentrated on driving——
'Your car!' she suddenly shrieked, startling both Flynn and his master.

'I put it in the garage while you were proving yourself a genius yet again in the kitchen.' He shook his head, laughing as she pulled a face at him. 'I'm serious,' he protested. 'There are professionals around not a patch on you.'

'A similar thought crossed my mind when I heard you playing the piano!' she exclaimed, remembering suddenly. 'I always thought that people as good as you are had to practise several hours a day—yet I've only heard you play once in the entire time I've been here.'

'I'd have to—to bring my playing up to scratch. I was described as exceptionally gifted as a child,' he replied, his completely matter-of-fact statement accompanied by the merest of dismissive shrugs. 'My interest in playing dwindled over the years.'

'Would you play for me now?' she asked, his slight hesitation instantly bringing back that feeling she had experienced of having touched a raw nerve in him that time his first dog had been mentioned.

'With pleasure,' he replied, rising.

She followed him into the drawing-room, Flynn close behind her, and was unable to shrug off a disturbing suspicion that pleasure was definitely not something he associated with his considerable gift.

He played for over an hour, constantly breaking off, then continuing only because she begged him to. Before each piece he would tell her its composer and its name or opus number.

'Liszt's "Hungarian Rhapsody Number One"— you probably know it,' he announced when she again begged him to carry on.

The name of the piece had meant nothing to her, but recognition came to her the instant his fingers began striking the notes, the breath catching in her throat as she acknowledged a brilliance in his playing that even an ear as untutored as hers could not fail to recognise.

'Oh, no!' she wailed in protest when the ringing of the telephone jarred through the last of those mesmerising notes. 'I'll get it.'

'And I'll put some coffee on,' he declared, firmly closing the lid of the piano as she dashed into the hall.

'Hi, there, Jane—it's Paul.'

'Paul—how are you? How's the holiday going?' she asked in a startled rush, conscious of the fact that she hadn't given him a single thought since last seeing him.

'Fine—listen, Jane, I have to see you. Are you free?'

'When?' she asked, frantically stalling and acutely conscious of Daniel standing in the doorway and making no attempt to disguise the fact that he was watching and listening.

'Now—it'll have to be right now as I'm off to Geneva first thing in the morning.'

'I really am sorry, Paul, but I can't——'

'Jane, I think you ought to find the time—this is important.'

'I'm sorry, Paul, but I really can't. In fact, I have to go now—I've left something unattended on the cooker.'

She felt only the merest twinge of guilt as she replaced the receiver. The urgency in Paul's tone was something she had come to recognise only too well in those days when he was trying to pressurise her into a relationship she simply wasn't prepared to accept. She had hoped all that was behind them. . .but that all too familiar tone seemed to tell her otherwise.

She started as she felt Daniel's hand on her shoulder. He turned her slowly, then took her into his arms.

'Liar,' he whispered huskily, burying his face in her hair. 'You should simply have told him your lover was on the verge of throwing a jealous fit.'

'That's a lie he might have had difficulty in swallowing,' she replied, her instinctive attempt to make the words light failing as they came out strained and breathless.

'I wish it were a lie—it's a feeling I detest. But I'm very glad you said all the right things.'

She buried her face against him, not daring to speak and reminding herself that he had expressed feelings of jealousy because of Paul once before. . .and then she most certainly hadn't taken it as tantamount to a declaration of love.

'Shall I make some coffee now?' he whispered, his breath soft against her ear.

She shook her head and he chuckled, his arms tightening around her. 'What would you have done,' she couldn't stop herself asking, 'if I'd agreed to meet Paul?'

'I'd probably have played the piano like a dervish all night.'

'You'd what?' she croaked, drawing back from him in surprise.

'That was one of the reasons I stopped playing. . . I'd come to use it as an outlet for my anger, and that's a criminal use of something as beautiful as music.'

'You were angry that first time I heard you play,' she remembered aloud, disturbed not so much by what he had said but by how much she intuitively knew he was leaving unsaid.

'But I wasn't angry this evening,' he protested laughingly, rubbing his nose against hers.

'But to feel you had to give it up as a child——'

'Jane, there's no need to make a big production out of it!' he exclaimed. 'I was simply a moody child who used the piano as an outlet for my moods until I realised it wasn't such a good idea. And anyway, I'm a big boy now—so what does it matter?'

Jane buried her face against him once more, hugging him tightly. It mattered very much to her. The little he had so reluctantly revealed to her of his childhood had painted her a picture of bleakness and solitude, and because she loved the man there was a part of her that suffered on behalf of the child.

'Hey,' he whispered softly, his lips nuzzling against her cheek, 'you're almost breaking my ribs. . . Let's take ourselves off somewhere more comfortable, where you can break them at your leisure.'

'I've just had Jacky on the line again,' announced Lyn appearing in the doorway of Jane's office. 'You're wanted at some sort of meeting in the boardroom.'

'Did she say what it was about?' asked Jane, her expression puzzled as she got to her feet. First the message to say that Daniel couldn't meet her for

lunch as arranged—again through Jacky—and now
this summons to a meeting out of the blue.

'Jacky says she's been trying to puzzle out what's
been going on all day,' replied Lyn. 'Apparently
Danny Boy's been closeted in his office all day—with
directors and company solicitors traipsing in and out
in their droves. . . Heavens, you don't suppose some
multi-billion-dollar concern is trying to take us over,
do you?'

'No, I don't,' chuckled Jane. 'But I'd better dash.'
She was already in the corridor when she gave a
sudden exclamation and darted back in and gave Lyn
a quick hug. 'Just in case this goes on for some
time—have a lovely holiday. And you might as well
slip off now—you probably haven't even started your
packing yet, if I know you!'

She paused momentarily outside the boardroom
and wondered if the day would ever come when she
would step through that door without that vague
feeling of being an impostor.

She walked in, her eyes widening in surprise
before she turned and carefully closed the door
behind her. Who *were* all these people?

'Ah—there you are, Miss Ashford,' exclaimed the
tall, patrician man making his way towards her.

Relieved to see a face she recognised, Jane smiled,
her mind racing to place him as he approached.
There were some of the directors she was still unable
to put a name to, but this one she could: Eric Shore,
and, if she remembered rightly, his field was inter-
national finance.

'We might as well sit ourselves here,' he murmured, choosing seats nearest the door and furthest
from the rest of those seated around the huge rectan-
gular table.

Not feeling confident enough to risk asking her
companion what all this was about, Jane sat down,

conscious of the unease growing in her. Daniel was seated at the head of the table, deep in conversation with another of the directors and a man she recognised as one of the company's solicitors. He appeared not to have noticed her arrival. Two more of the directors were seated around the head of the table, but the other six men, a little further down, were complete strangers to her. All of them had notebooks on the table in front of them and three of them were engrossed in writing in theirs.

'Right, we might as well recap and make sure no one's missed anything,' stated Daniel suddenly.

As the room fell silent, so the feeling of unease in Jane grew. Though he hadn't acknowledged her by so much as a glance, she was certain he was aware of her presence.

'You're probably finding all this as much a waste of your time as I do of mine,' he continued, 'but you can thank that section of your profession accurately referred to as the "gutter Press" for that—none of which, you may have noticed, has been asked along here.' His last observation was met with muted laughter. 'As you all know, Miss Ashford—who has now joined us—inherited my late grandmother's fifty-per-cent holding in the company.'

Jane's bewildered attempts to assimilate what little she was able to glean from his words froze in her mind as at least six pairs of eyes became trained on her.

'During her lifetime, my grandmother signed over total executive control of her shares to me—as has Miss Ashford.'

With several pairs of eyes still on her, Jane was beginning to feel like an animal in a zoo.

'Miss Ashford?' queried one of the men she now knew to be journalists.

For an instant she felt every nerve in her body

freeze, then she managed a reply. 'What Mr Blake says is perfectly correct.' She only just prevented herself from adding a plea for someone to explain to her what was going on.

'The document concerned is available for inspection should any of you feel the need,' continued Daniel in tones into which was creeping an element of boredom, while the solicitor beside him held a document aloft.

'So what's your problem, Blake?' asked one of the journalists. 'It's not as though this were a story that any of the qualities would carry—certainly not the financial Press.'

'Try telling that to your colleague on your left,' replied Daniel icily. 'Or haven't you seen the midday edition of his paper?'

'Come on, Blake, it was purely tongue-in-cheek,' protested the journalist concerned, with a somewhat sheepish smile.

'Tongue-in-cheek it might have been, but it also speculated on the possible repercussions on this company were someone of Miss Ashford's patent inexperience to try dabbling in the running of it,' pointed out Daniel frigidly.

'That was intended as pure farce—as well you know!' exclaimed the man, then raised his hands in a placating gesture as he was treated to a glacial stare. 'OK, we'll run a full cover on the facts—front page, all editions tomorrow.'

One of the other journalists caught Jane's eye. 'Miss Ashford, what have you to say——?'

'As I've already explained,' cut in Daniel sharply, 'Miss Ashford was so upset by all this that it took some persuading even to get her into the same room as a group of Pressmen. If you wish to ask any more questions, the company solicitor will deal with them.'

He rose. 'Now, if you'll excuse me, gentlemen, I have a business to run.'

Jane watched as he turned and had a word with one of the directors. Her head was reeling and she felt slightly sick—a feeling that increased alarmingly as he then strode down the length of the room, pausing as he reached her.

'Miss Ashford,' he murmured, his pleasant and unhurried tone in complete contrast to the steely pressure of the hand that took her arm and urged her to her feet.

With no option but to do so, Jane followed him from the room, her mind torn between a desperate need to make some sense of what had just happened and its immediate preoccupation with the hostile pressure of the fingers on her arm.

'Daniel, what——?'

'I'd rather you didn't say a word until we are in my office,' he snapped, releasing his hold on her and striding ahead so fast that she would have had to run to keep up with him.

Too stunned even to be capable of anger, she followed, the distance between them lengthening as she tried to piece together and make some sense of what had taken place.

'Daniel,' she began, as he closed the door behind them once she had caught up with him in his office.

'When exactly was it you held your Press conference?' he asked, his voice hoarse with barely suppressed fury. 'I suppose it had to be yesterday.'

Jane leaned against the closed door, the colour suddenly draining from her face. She had been so confused, so completely disorientated, that she had actually sat in a room full of reporters. . .and not once had her mind made any connection with yesterday's telephone call from. . .what was the woman's name?

'Polly Nestor,' she croaked in answer to her own question. 'Daniel, I just didn't get around to telling you——'

'What didn't you get around to telling me?' he demanded softly. 'Surely it wasn't your decision to try to get some pathetic measure of revenge against the Blakes at long last?'

This wasn't fair, she protested to herself in stunned bewilderment; her mind was being bombarded by one shock after another, with no time in between for her to get her bearings.

'And it really was a most pathetic measure,' he continued harshly, 'considering that all I had to do to counter it was prove you'd signed over all executive powers to me.'

Her mind had seized up on her completely, she thought frantically as she watched him stroll over to his desk and pick up one of the several newspapers strewn across its top.

'I can't say this is a rag I'm familiar with,' he drawled, gazing down at it, 'but no doubt you are—though I'll refresh your memory anyway.

"I've no intention of signing over my powers to anyone," declared the spunky blonde grand-daughter of the aforementioned Joe Marley.

"Oh, no, of course we haven't divided up the house," murmured the gorgeous Jane with a sexy little laugh that managed to imply volumes. "I'm living with one of the most eligible bachelors around and intend doing everything I can to keep it that way—permanently." As Jane has recently confided in a close friend that the outrageously attractive Daniel Blake is on the look-out for a wife, one wonders how soon wedding bells can be expected. And what more delightful way to put an end to that bitter family feud?

'There's quite a bit more in the same intellectual vein—but then, you don't need me to tell you that, do you?' he drawled coldly, letting the paper drop from his hands as though they had been contaminated by it.

Jane felt herself straighten suddenly, and what staggered her—more than anything she was hearing and even more than the realisation that the man she loved had just condemned her totally out of hand— was the inexplicable calmness she was experiencing. That it was almost guaranteed to be that unnatural calm which came before a storm didn't even enter her head—she was in control of herself and for that she was inordinately grateful.

'Daniel, it obviously hasn't even occurred to you that I might have been grossly misquoted,' she stated quietly.

'I wouldn't chance your luck, if I were you,' he warned her softly, his hands clenching visibly at his sides. 'You threatened me with the Press—remember? Though, God knows, even I didn't realise you were stupid enough to think such a threat could pack any punch once you'd signed all your powers over to me.'

Jane felt the calm she had so welcomed begin to disintegrate within her.

'And you always believe what you read in the Press, is that it, Daniel?' she asked, her voice no longer steady.

She had to steel herself from cringing against the door as he suddenly marched over to her.

'You disappoint me, Jane,' he murmured, stopping just short of her. 'Even though your naïve attempt to wreak revenge on the Blakes has backfired so miserably, I thought you'd at least have the guts to come out and admit you tried.' His eyes swept over her in disgust. 'And as for believing what I read in the papers, there are certain facts in that garbage which are known only to you and to me. . .or do you intend making an even bigger fool of yourself by denying that too?'

'You're right, of course, Daniel; a fool such as I am would only be wasting her time trying to pull the wool over the eyes of someone as clever as you,' she replied, the bravura of defiance in her words as she felt the last tenuous flicker die in her of what had never been more than a tiny spark of hope.

'That's more like it,' he drawled, his eyes chips of ice as he suddenly reached out and pulled her against him. 'Why struggle, Jane?' he laughed derisively as she began fighting him like one possessed. 'You had your little go at revenge and it fell flat on you. But nothing's really changed, has it? My aim is still to get you out of the house and, ultimately, the business.'

It was almost as though she recognised those words hitting her ears like piercing slivers of ice, the words she had for so long lived in dread of hearing, yet had foolishly allowed herself to begin hoping she might never hear.

He lowered his head to hers, his mouth softly coaxing against her ear. 'And I'm sure you want me out of your blood,' he whispered, 'every bit as much as I want you out of mine.'

As his arms drew her even closer she was unsure which startled her more—the swift surge of desire in the lean body trapping hers or the uninhibited violence of the need with which her own instantly responded.

'How could you possibly want someone you believe has just tried to stab you in the back?' she choked, unable to stop the words.

'And how can you possibly want someone you've just tried to stab in the back?' he countered, suddenly releasing her and walking away from her. 'But you do. . .we both do.'

CHAPTER TEN

DANIEL was sitting on her bed, a dark blue bathrobe belted around him, when Jane entered her room from the bathroom late that evening.

'This is my room—get out of it!' she rounded on him, her hands flying to the towel around her damp body, her fingers shaking as they secured it more firmly around her.

'You could have showered with me—in our bathroom,' he taunted, the glint of desire already creeping into the eyes making their leisurely inspection of her still-glistening body. 'There's nothing to be gained from playing hard to get at this late stage, now, is there, darling?' he drawled, rising and walking towards her.

'Don't call me darling,' she objected, her teeth clenching tightly as she closed her eyes to the hypnotic message emanating from his as he drew closer.

'I'll call you what the hell I like,' he informed her harshly. 'And must you really resort to the ridiculous ploy of closing your eyes? You know it never gets you anywhere.'

'Get out of here,' she chanted tonelessly, the tingling awareness already prickling against her skin warning her that the leaden feeling of deadness which had so perturbed her until now was about to desert her at the one time she would have welcomed it.

'The day you say that and mean it—I'll leave,' he told her, placing his hands on her shoulders, his fingers playing lightly against her skin. 'And you want that day to come as much as I do, don't you,

Jane?' he coaxed softly. 'The day when we'll both be free of this maddening need for one another?'

It took every ounce of strength she possessed to prevent herself from shaking her head. She would never be free.

'The fact that you've at last showed your hand alters nothing; you were bound to do so sooner or later.'

'And the thought that I would never bothered you?' she asked bitterly, humiliation flooding her as she remembered how she had actually almost fooled herself into believing his desire could be love.

'Why should it? We've always been sexually honest with one another and that's all that's ever mattered between us. . .and all that ever will until this need afflicting us has burned itself out.'

She forced her body to become limp as he began drawing her into his arms, but she knew she was fighting a losing battle, not only against her own insatiable longing, but also because by resisting it was almost as though she was admitting she never wanted him to be free of needing her.

'Put your arms round me,' he urged huskily, removing the towel from around her as his lips brushed seductively against hers.

She shook her head, uncertain what it was she was denying as her arms crept around him and he lifted her off her feet.

'Don't ever say no to me unless you mean it,' he whispered, his lips hot and demanding against hers, 'because all I have to do is to take you in my arms to discover the truth.'

And this time it was her body that fought his in the hope of finding once more the tenderness it now craved; but this time it was tenderness that lost out to the tempestuous madness which finally consumed them both. And when that madness was spent there was only the aching void of loneliness in her and the bitter-sweet memory of the laughter and tenderness that were no more.

In the waxy paleness of the moonlight, she gazed down at the sleeping man beside her, his back turned towards her as he rejected her even in sleep. She drew herself up into a half-sitting position against the pillows, the still silence of the night offering a measure of ease to the tortured confusion that had raged for so long within her.

It wasn't simply the mind-numbing events of today that had so stupefied her that she was incapable of stringing together a single coherent thought, she told herself: the Jane Ashford of old, the once rational, intelligent and fun-loving person she had developed into over the years, had begun changing almost from the day Dolly Blake's fateful will had been read. Perhaps she *had* grossly underestimated the power of the attraction that had first drawn her to Daniel and had lain semi-dormant in her over all those years. But that girl who had once yearned for him from afar would never in a thousand years have allowed herself to become reduced to little more than a slave to her body's insatiable need for a man whose only wish was to be rid of her. Perhaps that person she had once been would have been just as easily fooled by the practised duplicity of a Polly Nestor—but she certainly would never have allowed herself to be subjected to the ghastly events of today without putting up a fight; and she would have gone on fighting until there was no shred of doubt left as to her innocence.

'I'll show you, Daniel Blake!' she cried out in the voice of her old self. 'I'll show you,' she repeated stubbornly, as another voice demanded to know how.

He turned as she spoke that second time, his eyes

half opening and his expression gentled by the sleep still claiming him as he murmured her name.

'Where are you?' he complained drowsily, drawing her down beside him and nestling his head against her breasts.

Proving her innocence to him wasn't the most important consideration in her life, she accepted dejectedly as her arms curved in love around his sleeping form; she would quite happily accept his believing her to be a mass murderer if only she could rid herself of loving him.

'Hi, Jane—haven't seen you in ages,' called out Mary Leigh as Jane entered the main office of the company's advertising section.

'Lyn's on holiday,' smiled Jane. 'Need I say more?'

Mary laughed sympathetically and began clearing a space on her cluttered desk. 'Take a pew. I'm sure you could squeeze in a quick coffee—I'm dying for one, though I must say you look as though you could do with something stronger.'

'A very quick coffee will do nicely,' said Jane, taking a seat and immediately sensing the relaxed atmosphere in the office, despite the frantic hive of industry that buzzed constantly in it. The atmosphere was as it was because Joan Sellers was no longer a part of it, she suddenly realised.

'Jane, I know it's a dreadful thing to say to someone. . .' Mary frowned as she handed her a mug of coffee '. . .but you do look pretty rough—are you OK?'

Jane took a hasty sip of the drink; she was all too aware of how ghastly she looked—even Daniel had remarked on it that morning.

'I had a bit of a headache earlier,' she lied off the top of her head, 'but I'm fine now.'

Mary gave her a slightly doubting look, then

smiled. 'So—what can I do for you, or is this a purely social visit?'

Jane returned her smile as she shook her head. 'Actually, I came to ask you about the temp you have working here—the one due to finish today. Was she any good?'

'Sally? She's a little treasure—in fact, I was going to have a word with you about her,' said Mary. 'She was wondering if any of the other departments might need her—though what she'd really like is a permanent job here if something comes up.'

'So she wouldn't mind temping in personnel for a while?'

'She'd jump at it,' laughed Mary. 'I've just sent her off to the printer with some copy, but I'll have a word with her when she gets back.'

'If you're sure that will be OK with her I'll get on to her agency,' said Jane, relieved.

'I'm positive,' Mary assured her. 'Sally's. . . Oh, lord—trouble!'

Jane turned, just in time to see Joan Sellers approaching.

I'd like these back within the next half-hour—I need to check them over the weekend,' said Joan, dropping a large portfolio of work on Mary's desk.

'So nice to see you, Joan,' murmured Mary drily, as the woman turned to leave.

It was as Mary spoke that Jane glanced up and caught Joan's eye. It was the almost imperceptible stiffening in her expression, together with a faint, yet unmistakable reddening of her cheeks that triggered off a welter of sensations in Jane. . .for no apparent reason, Joan was totally nonplussed.

'I haven't seen you for some time, Joan,' she remarked quietly, the sensations co-ordinating themselves into what became almost a certainty in her mind. 'And how is your cousin Katrina?'

The look of pure malevolence to which she was subjected, before Joan turned and marched from the room without uttering another word, rendered Jane's certainty complete.

'My word, if looks could kill!' breathed Mary, plainly somewhat puzzled. 'And, whatever that was all about, I'd watch that woman. She's been after your blood ever since you had her isolated from the rest of this department.'

'That was Daniel's decision,' muttered Jane, barely conscious of having uttered the words, so preoccupied was she by what was taking place in her mind.

'Yes, but it was all thanks to you—for which we're all eternally grateful to you,' stated Mary. 'But I mean it—watch her. I'm afraid I'm not the only one who thinks there's something unbalanced about that woman—no matter how good she may be at her job.'

Jane finished her coffee and left. She felt drained and shivery as she returned to her office. Unbalanced was the only word to describe the mind that had engineered that ghastly article appearing in the Press. . .and she knew with an unshakeable certainty that that mind had been Joan's.

She rang the temping agency, the question of how Joan had obtained the information she had remaining unanswered in her mind. The question why was one she found too disturbing to contemplate. . .it was a question only a mind as unbalanced as Joan's could ever answer.

Yet Joan's name had never even entered her head during those long silent hours of the night during which her thoughts were at their clearest. It was during those hours, when all passion was spent and the stranger she loved lay sleeping in her arms, that she had accepted that she had lost and must give Daniel what he had always demanded. She knew she could not leave the house without leaving the company at the same time, because she trusted neither herself nor him to handle even the most public of meetings while that insatiable hunger still raged on unassuaged between them. She had accepted being unable to leave while Lyn was absent, but she had quietly made her plans.

And now this, she agonised, her mind bruised by shock. In one deranged moment of despair she had actually considered Lyn as a possible—though unwitting—culprit; then Paul French. She let out a low groan as she remembered Paul's attempt to speak to her. . .to warn her, most probably!

She reached for the telephone, her hand shaking as she dialled the number of Paul's paper. For all she knew his holiday was over and he had left the country for good.

'Hello, I——'

'Would you mind holding on one moment?' came the operator's brisk voice.

The look of resignation on her face switched to one of horror as the door of her office opened and Daniel strolled into the room. She trained her gaze on the desk-top before her, silently telling herself to be calm, that there was no way he could know.

'Hello—who did you wish to speak to?'

'Paul French—he's one of your overseas correspondents——'

'Mr French doesn't work from these premises.'

'I realise that, but I need to contact him,' explained Jane, acutely aware of Daniel's glowering presence. 'Haven't you a number for him in England?'

'The only thing I can suggest is that you leave your name and number and I can give him them if he calls in here.'

'No—it doesn't matter,' muttered Jane despondently—the last thing she intended doing was giving out her telephone number with Daniel standing there beside her, listening without shame to her every word.

'Having problems with your paper-boy?' he enquired with sugary sweetness, as she replaced the receiver. 'You can hardly blame him, though, can you? There are few men around prepared to take another man's cast-offs,' he taunted. 'And, besides, I haven't finished with you yet.'

The vicious coldness of these words, coming from the man whose arms held her in tempestuous passion night after night, snapped something within her.

'And what about Katrina?' she retaliated. 'Will she be prepared to have you back when I've finished with you?'

'Your knowing her name is something that intrigued me once before—it still does. You seem to have been playing detective, Jane. . . I wonder why.'

'Well, you can stop wondering. She happens to be the cousin of one of your most popular employees—Joan Sellers,' she retorted. 'I'd be grateful if you'd say whatever it is you came here to say—I have work to get on with.'

'I came to say I'm going out and shan't be in for supper this evening. . .though whether or not I shall be unfaithful to you tonight remains to be seen.'

Though she felt certain that that remark had been prompted by his fury over hearing her try to contact Paul, it did nothing to lessen the ferocity of the pain with which it hit her.

'You really can't face the idea of my being unfaithful to you, can you?' he murmured, his eyes curiously devoid of the mockery she had expected in them as he leaned back against her desk-top and gazed down at her.

'Perhaps not now,' she replied, stunned when she

heard the reckless candour of her words. 'But soon it won't matter in the least to me.'

'Soon?' he asked softly; then, when she made no reply, he added in that same, almost gentle voice, 'I shan't be very late tonight.'

He straightened, then suddenly held out his hand to her, a gesture unlike any he had made towards her during the relentless hostility of the past week.

She took his hand because she couldn't stop herself; she was unable to leave him without saying her own silent goodbye.

When he drew her towards him she entered his arms willingly, and when he kissed her she responded with the simplicity of love; and she saw the look of disquiet on his face when that kiss finally ended.

'Jane,' he muttered hoarsely, 'you're up to something.'

She gave him a gentle push towards the door, conscious of the glitter of unshed tears in her eyes.

'Yes—I'm trying to get rid of you. I've work to finish.'

He turned as he reached the door. 'Something warns me you're about to try stabbing me in the back once more,' he said in a quiet, oddly hesitant voice.

She was glad of the bitterness that filled her with those words—they were a reminder to her that she had taken the only decision available to her.

'Why would I even both trying,' she asked wearily, 'when the last attempt failed so miserably? Though I'm not so sure Katrina's cousin would agree.'

It was only when she heard the outer door close behind him that a shuddering sigh escaped her and her tears ran free. He hadn't even taken her up on her remark about Joan, she told herself bitterly. His certainty regarding her guilt was impregnable—a sledge-hammer would have made no more impression on him than that foolishly subtle hint she should have known better than to hold out to him.

She went to her desk and took out the letter she had written Lyn, her gaze straying towards the telephone. She shook her head: there was no point trying to contact Paul. It simply didn't matter any more. That chapter of her life was now closing behind her forever.

CHAPTER ELEVEN

'JANE, where are you, for goodness sake?' gasped Lyn. 'It's been almost two weeks and I've been half out of my mind with worry!'

'I explained it all in my letter,' said Jane, her heart in her mouth—she should never have rung!

'Damn that letter!' exploded Lyn, plainly close to tears. 'It was nothing but a pack of lies!'

'Lyn, I needed a holiday——'

'Danny Boy's been tearing his hair out. He practically beat me up the day I got back——'

'Lyn, please——'

'He was convinced I'd know where you are. Jane, where the hell *are* you?'

'Lyn, I'll explain—can you meet me at that coffee-shop we used to go to?'

'The one with the special cakes?'

'Yes; I'll meet you there when you've finished work—in about a quarter of an hour?'

'I'll be there.'

'And, Lyn—I hate to put it like this, but I'll never forgive you if you mention a word of this to anyone—especially Daniel.'

'I'll have to let John know,' protested Lyn. 'That's another thing,' she added bitterly, 'we got engaged when I came back from my holiday.'

'Oh, Lyn, I'm so thrilled to hear that——'

'You could have heard it a lot sooner if only you'd contacted me,' accused Lyn.

'I'll see you in about fifteen minutes,' said Jane and with shaking hands replaced the receiver.

She took a deep breath to try to counteract the

trembling now racking through her, realising just how much simply making the call had taken out of her.

She slipped on her jacket and closed behind her the door of the small service flat she had rented for a month, knowing that the entire time she had been speaking to Lyn her mind had been elsewhere—in that office on the top floor of the building in which she had pictured the man whose image had never once left her thoughts during these past days of grinding loneliness and despair.

And there was guilt in her as she made her way to meet her closest friend, as she had to admit it wasn't so much their friendship that drew her towards Lyn as Lyn's proximity to the man she still craved with the single-mindedness of an addict.

She had tried kidding herself that re-establishing contact with Lyn would be a step towards rebuilding her shattered life. . .yet it was her craving for even the most tenuous of second-hand contacts with Daniel that now guided her steps.

'I shouldn't have had a go at you like that on the phone,' choked Lyn, as they hugged each other in greeting. 'But you've no idea how worried I've been.'

'Lyn—I'm so sorry,' Jane apologised huskily. 'Everything just got on top of me.'

They sat down and gave the waiter their order.

'It was that damned Press report, wasn't it?' Lyn asked bitterly once the waiter had gone.

Jane nodded. 'I wasn't too sure if you'd have heard about it.'

'Jacky told me about it the moment I got back— you realise Danny Boy's fired her.'

Jane looked at her in bewilderment, unsure that she had heard correctly. 'Why on earth would he fire Jacky?'

'Not Jacky!' retorted Lyn impatiently. 'That Sellers creature.'

Jane felt her head begin to swim, and when the waiter appeared with a pot of coffee and a selection of cakes she felt for one dreadful moment as though she was about to pass out.

'Why did he fire her?' she asked once the feeling had mercifully subsided, her voice barely recognisable.

'Because she was behind that Press leak,' replied Lyn, looking at her as though she was mad. 'For heaven's sake, Jane, if she wasn't the first and only person you suspected you need your head examined!'

'I only realised it was Joan the day I left,' whispered Jane hoarsely. 'And then it was only a gut feeling. . . I couldn't have proved anything. She knew all those things that no one else knew.'

'I knew them, and Danny Boy did too,' pointed out Lyn quietly. 'And, between us, he and I managed to work out exactly when it was she was able to eavesdrop on what.'

Jane looked at her dazedly. 'I'm surprised you got any help from him!' she then exclaimed bitterly. 'He was only too eager to judge and condemn me when it all happened.'

'Why the hell didn't you simply tell him the truth?' demanded Lyn.

'I did, but he wasn't interested,' retorted Jane, hurt by the open accusation in Lyn's tone. 'As I said, he was only too happy to believe the worst of me.'

'So why did he go chasing after people like Paul French?'

'Probably because he thought I'd moved in with Paul. . . I've no idea!' She gave a bitter laugh. 'It's funny, I had a hunch that Paul might have had some information on the subject.'

'So why didn't you contact him and find out what Danny Boy did?'

'I tried once. . .but then it didn't really seem to matter any more.'

'I'd say it probably matters more than anything else in your life,' stated Lyn quietly. 'Because you're just as in love with him as ever.'

'I'll get over it,' lied Jane, picking up a cake and gazing sightlessly at it as the loneliness and despair welled up in her with savage intensity. 'And you're wrong—there was a brief time when I'd have given anything to be able to prove my innocence to Daniel. . .but now it honestly doesn't matter to me one way or another.'

For several seconds Lyn said nothing, then she glanced at her watch and leapt to her feet. 'I nearly forgot—would you mind awfully if I tried contacting John again? I couldn't get through to him before I left work.'

Jane shook her head. 'And I want to hear all about your engagement when you get back.' She smiled. 'And when the wedding's to be.'

She watched with an exasperated smile as Lyn dashed through the door before she could catch her attention and remind her of the telephone almost behind them. She sat drinking her coffee, her heart warming at the thought of John and Lyn finally deciding to get married. And she had better get a firm grip on herself before Lyn returned—in her selfishness she had already marred Lyn's happiness enough as it was.

She gave a sudden start as she felt something brush against her leg, all her resolutions about getting a grip on herself falling by the wayside as the unexpected sensation started memories tugging at her heart. It had felt just like Flynn's silken coat brushing against her, she realised, looking around almost furtively—the management would have a fit if they discovered a dog had strolled in, as the snuffling rumpus by her feet seemed to indicate. She pushed back her chair and peered under the table.

Stretched out at her feet, his head on his paws, lay Flynn, his soulful brown eyes gazing up at her adoringly.

'It can't be you, darling!' she croaked in disbelief, reaching down her hand to receive those familiar ecstatic licks while her heart raced suffocatingly out of control.

'Madam, dogs aren't allowed on these premises!' hissed the waiter, who had rushed to the table.

'I. . . I'm sorry. . .he must have followed me in,' stammered Jane dazedly, leaping to her feet and hastily handing him money to cover the order. 'Come along, Flynn,' she whispered, 'before you get me into any more trouble.'

She dashed from the coffee-house, the dog keeping so close to her side he was almost leaning on her. Once in the street she simply let her instincts take over; she sank to her knees and flung her arms around him.

'You'll never know how much I've missed you!' she cried, burying her head against his golden coat as he made soft growling sounds of contentment.

'I doubt if it's as much as he's missed you,' remarked the voice she would recognise till the day she died.

Panic-stricken, she leapt to her feet, gazing around her in trapped confusion in search of Lyn. The panic eased almost as suddenly as it had gripped her as she realised she was searching in vain for the friend who had so obviously betrayed her.

'Jane, you mustn't think too badly of Lyn,' that same voice cautioned her. 'She knew how desperate I was to speak to you.'

It was then that she could no longer keep her eyes from turning towards Daniel, and when they did she couldn't prevent the sharp gasp of horror that escaped her when she saw the change in his appearance. His was a face that would always look handsome, no matter how ravaged, and now it was verging on that: drawn, almost haggard—a face reflecting the desperation with which he had claimed to need to speak to her.

'Daniel, you look terrible,' she gasped before she had a chance to bite back the words.

'I can't say I feel too good,' he murmured wryly, suddenly dragging his fingers through his hair in an odd mixture of perplexity and impatience. 'Jane, could we go somewhere else and talk?'

'No!' She shook her head vehemently.

'Jane, please. . . I need you to sign some papers in connection with the company.'

'Why can't you do that?' she protested, not believing him and not believing, either, the devastating effect just seeing him was having on her. 'I've signed any powers I had over to you.'

'But you're still co-owner of the company; your signature will still be required from time to time. Please, Jane.'

Unable to trust herself to speak, she gave a helpless shrug, whereupon he immediately opened the passenger-door of his car for her.

She climbed in, steeling herself against the memories of other times as Flynn leapt into the bucket-seat behind her and rested his head on her shoulder.

'Hello, my darling,' she whispered to him, a riot of memories aching their way throughout her.

'He went missing the Monday after you left,' Daniel told her as he started up the car. 'I've a feeling that, with you gone and with me back at the office, he decided that we'd both abandoned him.'

'How long was he gone—where did you find him?' she asked, horrified.

'I didn't find him till about eleven that night— loitering by the park, weren't you, you big softie?' he accused the dog.

'Thank heavens he was all right,' muttered Jane, scratching her fingers against a silky ear.

'He's all right. But what about you? Jane, I suppose it's pointless my asking if you'll ever be able to forgive me.'

Completely thrown by both his words and their tone, she found herself struggling for words.

'What's there to forgive, really?' she managed eventually—she could hardly blame him for the fact that she loved him, she reasoned half-heartedly. 'It was only natural that you should resent me because of your grandmother's will. . .and, as you so rightly pointed out, I had threatened you with the Press.'

She closed her eyes as they turned into the drive, unable to bear the sight of the lovely house that had come to mean so much to her without her ever fully realising it.

But she found the memories assailing her almost too much for her as they entered the house.

'I'll put some coffee on,' he offered in that formal, almost strained voice that had once so troubled her.

She followed him into the kitchen, her heart threatening to break when Flynn began bounding in and out of the utility-room until eventually every soft toy he possessed lay at her feet.

'Would you mind if I fed him?' she asked, her voice tight with the threat of tears as the dog finally padded up to her and presented her with his bowl.

'No—he'd love that,' replied Daniel, his back to her as he prepared the coffee, then added suddenly, 'I fired Joan Sellers.'

'I know—Lyn told me,' she replied, completely thrown by the unexpectedness of his statement.

'She's threatening me with an unfair-dismissal suit.'

'Does that worry you?'

'I'd have hoped you knew me better than to have asked.'

Of course she knew him better, she told herself—this time finding herself thrown that he should express a hope that she did.

'So. . .you can come back to work now.'

Jane finished preparing Flynn's food—her heart hammering.

'I didn't leave because of Joan,' she told him unsteadily, then took the bowl to the patio.

'No,' he said, taking the coffee to the table. 'Perhaps I should show you that document before we have this,' he suggested stiltedly.

She would sign it and leave, she vowed to herself—she couldn't take much more of this. She followed him into one of the sitting-rooms, love like a greed in her eyes as they clung to the tall familiar figure walking to the bureau and taking from it a large envelope.

'Jane, could I just ask you one thing?' he asked, tossing the envelope down on to a chair and striding to her.

When he placed his hands on her shoulders she screwed her eyes shut as the familiar longings surged through her, as powerful and potent as they had ever been.

'I want to sign whatever it is and go,' she protested in a choking, breathless voice.

'Did you leave because you no longer wanted me?' he demanded harshly.

'Yes!'

'So why are your eyes closed, Jane? Why are you

having to fight that same battle with yourself you always do?' His lips, hungry and impatient, were on hers almost before he had finished those accusing words, and before he had finished drawing her fully into his arms. 'Tell me that you've missed me as much as I've missed you,' he pleaded, almost choking her with the suffocating fierceness of his hold as her arms crept up to wind around his neck as though they never again intended releasing him. 'Tell me,' he insisted hoarsely.

'Of course I missed you,' she raged brokenly, her lips as hungry as his in that instant before she began fighting the insanity about to possess her completely. 'And I'll just have to go on mising you,' she hurled at him, her voice rising uncontrollably, 'because I've no intention of subjecting myself to. . .to such humiliation again!'

'Humiliation?' he gasped, releasing her instantly. 'Jane, when two people want one another with the same intensity we do, how can either of them possibly feel humiliated by it?'

'Because. . .because I. . . Daniel, please, just let me sign whatever it is and go!'

He took the document from the envelope and handed it to her. 'You'll have to read it.'

'All I want to do is sign it!'

'You'll have to read it to find out where it needs signing,' he insisted stubbornly, turning his back on her and ramming his hands into his pockets.

Conscious that he was deliberately stalling, she began reading. After a few moments she stumbled towards a chair and sat down on it.

'Daniel, is this meant to be some sort of joke?' she asked hoarsely.

'Until each of us has children, we are the only ones to whom the house can belong, either singly or jointly. I'm signing my share over to you—I can't see any joke to be found in that,' he informed her coolly.

'But. . . Daniel, why?'

'Does there have to be a reason why? Just accept it—together with my apologies for the way I treated you.'

'But you love this house,' she protested.

'Do I?' he asked with bitter irony. 'It's the only home I've ever known—though hardly the most stable and secure from a child's point of view.' He strolled over to the sofa and flung himself down on it, a bitter half-smile on his lips as he gazed over at her. 'They say that home is where the heart is, don't they? Well, mine is no longer here. . .so it's all yours and I wish you luck in finding happiness in it.'

'Something you never did find here,' she stated quietly, the image of that lonely child he had once been returning to haunt her.

He shrugged. 'Perhaps I never looked hard enough for it—perhaps I simply didn't recognise it. My grandfather was an eccentric enough character to fascinate a child—though whether he engendered happiness is another matter. And it's only since I've delved into my grandmother's diaries that I've come to realise how much more there was to her than that rather vague and often scatty exterior of hers. As for my parents. . .the only thing I learned from them was how ephemeral happiness is. . .though I'm prepared to concede they weren't the best teachers to be taking lessons from.'

'Daniel, if the house means so little to you why were you so determined to get me out of it?' she asked, wondering now, as she had so often before, how it was she had come to love a man she found so impossible to understand.

His eyes met hers, an oddly questioning wariness in their depths.

'I'd have thought you'd have worked that out for yourself by now,' he challenged.

With a barely stifled exclamation of exasperation, Jane got to her feet. It had only been her foolish imagination that had tricked her into believing that for a few brief moments of magic she had been close to the real man behind the impenetrable surface. Now she could only accept that the wall he had erected around himself was one he had no intention of ever letting anyone penetrate—especially not her.

'I have to go now,' she stated stiffly. 'I'd just like to say that I understand how badly your grandmother's legacy to me must have disrupted your life, and that I'm sorry. I've also always regretted not apologising to you for the vicious tirade against the Blakes with which I repaid your kindness in finally allowing me to understand what really happened between our grandfathers. The fact that I was so upset at the thought of what my father had suffered is absolutely no excuse for my turning on you like that. After that outburst, and with my already having foolishly threatened you with talking to the Press, your holding me responsible for the dreadful article was only too understandable.' Though she could hear the desperation creeping into her stilted rush of words, she knew she had to keep on until she was finished— only then would she be free to leave. 'And I'm sorry you feel as you do about the house, because it was always my intention to make it wholly yours. That's still my intention, if only because it's a place in which I could never feel happy again.'

'Why not?' he enquired.

The utter coldness with which he had spoken almost stifled the breath in her.

'I'd have thought you'd have worked that out for yourself,' she said, flinging his own words back at him.

'Jane, you said you could never be happy *again* in this house. . .which seems to imply you once were.'

'I must have expressed myself badly,' she retorted agitatedly, starting towards the door and praying her legs were not about to give way under her.

'For a while I felt that you were happy. . .and I've often wondered if you wouldn't have gone on being happy here had I not been so vociferous in my jealousy over Paul French. . .he was only trying to warn you what was about to break in the Press that night he rang.'

Jane reached the door and hung on to it while her mind flatly refused even to attempt examining his words.

'It would be rather ironic if my reasons for wanting you out of the house were the same as those causing your unhappiness in it,' he observed, rising and walking towards where she stood clinging to the door as though for support. 'I didn't want you here originally, because I couldn't trust myself not to fall in love with you. . . Jane, must you swing on the door like that?' he added almost irritably. 'You could drag it off its hinges.'

Jane clung even tighter to the door, her eyes wide with shock as her mind stirred itself momentarily, then lapsed back into non-co-operation.

'You're just trying to get me to admit that I love you,' she accused indignantly.

'There are some who might construe that you just had,' he pointed out quietly. 'Now—would you mind detaching yourself from that door before I really lose my reason altogether and start regarding it as a rival?'

'What?' she croaked inanely, now clinging to the door as though for her life as her mind struggled to start functioning again.

'Jane, I love you,' he informed her quietly. 'And

I'm trying to be very calm and collected about all this, but I'm afraid I'm not going to succeed for very much longer.'

'Did you just say that you love me?' she demanded warily, making no attempt to help as he prised her, with considerable difficulty, from her moorings and took her into his arms.

'I love you, all right,' he groaned, his lips soft and murmuring against her cheek as his arms tightened around her. 'I love you, and never in my worst nightmares did I imagine loving could be as ghastly as this.'

'Ghastly?' she shrieked, clinging to him with every bit as much fervour as she had to the door. 'It's only you who makes it so ghastly. It should be the most beautiful experience that anyone could ever——'

'And it is,' he protested distractedly. 'Jane, if you really do love me, would you for goodness' sake tell me?'

'If?' she gasped indignantly. 'I first had the misfortune of running into you when I was nineteen—I haven't been able to raise so much as a flicker of interest in another man since! I've loved you in every way it's possible for a woman to love a man—and you have the nerve to ask me if I love you?'

'I know, I have the most appalling nerve—but I'm still asking you,' he whispered softly.

She took a breath on which to vent even more of her indignation on him, and suddenly found that breath trapped in her by the strange and wondrous realisation now spreading through her. She was in the arms of the only man she ever could, ever would, love. . .and he had spoken the only words she had ever wanted to hear from him.

'Of course I love you,' she croaked in dazed indignation, her words husky with the threat of tears. 'I. . .of course I love you.'

He dropped his head to her shoulder, a groaned sigh shuddering through him.

'Jane, can you ever forgive me?' he begged hoarsely.

For several seconds she gazed down at the dark head pressed against her, her expression almost fearful as thoughts and sensations darted in a confusing jumble within her. Then suddenly the confusion was gone and she was filled with an indescribably beautiful sense of peace.

'For loving me?' she teased huskily, her hands reaching up to stroke against his hair as an excess of love threatened to spill from her every pore. 'No—never.'

'I'm serious,' he groaned, dragging her over to the sofa and pulling her down beside him. 'Jane, I don't want to bore you with the reasons why I was so. . . Hell, why not admit it?' he demanded angrily. 'Why I was so terrified of love.'

'I probably would have been too, if I'd had parents like yours as an example,' she pointed out gently.

'I honestly was never conscious of feeling that way, probably because, despite all the women I've known, the complication of falling in love had never arisen in my life until the day I stepped into a lift and found myself pulling out all the stops in order to attract the attention of the most fascinating bundle of unselfconscious beauty I'd ever clapped eyes on.' His arm drew her more securely against him. 'I'm not making any far-fetched claims to love as first sight. . .it's just that the image of you stayed with me as that of no other woman ever has. It was from the day I kissed you under the mistletoe that I realised I would love you if ever I allowed you to get too close.'

'And then your grandmother stepped in,' murmured Jane, suddenly loving Dolly Blake.

'Jane, it was always fear of loving—never any material consideration—that made me behave so appallingly towards you; it got to a stage where I found it almost impossible to communicate with you.'

'Was that why you became so. . .so polite and constrained whenever you spoke to me?'

'Do you think I couldn't hear how ghastly I sounded?' He groaned exasperatedly. 'I felt split in two—half of me wanting to keep you at a distance, the other half wanting to know that you loved me. I was the one who'd kept on about there being nothing more between us than a powerful sexual attraction. . .and then I couldn't quite convince myself that that wasn't all it actually was for you——'

'But you knew you were the only man who had ever made love to me,' she protested.

'I knew,' he sighed. 'Damn it, Jane, I'd never experienced anything as mind-blowing as loving before—the last thing I was capable of was rationality! I literally ran away from you when I took off for France out of the blue like that. . .because the last thing I was prepared to admit to myself at that point was that I loved you.' He hugged her to him in fierce desperation. 'Jane, my going with Katrina was pure fluke—she'd rung me to ask if she could use my place at Juan-les-Pins because she was going there on business. I told her she couldn't as I'd be using it myself. We arranged to travel there together. . . I'm afraid things got a little out of hand when she turned up at my place later that evening——'

'Daniel, you don't have to tell me all this,' she protested softly. 'It doesn't matter any more.'

'It mattered one hell of a lot to me!' he exclaimed morosely. 'Despite what I tried leading you to believe, no other woman meant anything to me from the moment you moved in here. I ran away from you like some pathetic wimp. . .and all I could think about, once I'd left, was how quickly I could get back to you. . . I thought it wasn't possible for me to be any more confused than I was then, though I found out it was when you left. Jane, for these past couple of weeks I've felt as though I was about to go insane!'

She reached up and kissed his cheek. 'That's all behind us now,' she whispered as he drew back with an impatient groan.

'But I can still feel it eating away inside me,' he protested, refusing to be consoled. 'Jane, things simply went from bad to worse for me once we became lovers—I got it into my head that if I actually came out with it and told you I loved you I might frighten you off, because part of me refused to believe you loved me in return. Yet something in me drove me to express my love for you in other ways.'

'By searching out Dolly's diaries,' she whispered sadly. 'And all I did was rant at you after you'd read them to me.'

'I asked for that by not having the guts to tell you I loved you and taking the risk of finding out you didn't love me in return. . . Hell, how could you possibly be expected to realise my programmed-robot routine was my way of trying to express love?' he asked disgustedly.

She scrabbled free of his arms, kneeling beside him and placing her own arms around his neck.

'I love you, my darling robot. . . I love you,' she insisted, half laughing, half crying.

'You actually love a man who is such a coward he even resorted to getting his dog to go in and fetch you out of that coffee-house?' he queried suspiciously.

'I actually do,' she breathed, her eyes luminous as they reflected the love they found shining so clearly in his.

He cupped her face in his hands, his eyes now bombarding her with love as what began as a reluctant smile of diffidence became transformed into a grin of total satisfaction that danced lazily across his features.

'I suppose—if you've got it that badly—there's even a chance that you'll marry me,' he teased

She twisted her face against his hands, her eyes closing, her lips kissing mutely against his palm as the thought entered her head that there was definitely a limit to the amount of happiness she was able to cope with at one go.

'Hey. . .don't you dare close your eyes on me now,' he protested with a soft chuckle. 'I've just asked you to marry me and I want an answer.'

'I didn't know it was possible to feel this happy,' she choked.

'I'm pleased to hear it,' he replied. 'But I'd be even more pleased if you answered my question.'

'Of course I'll marry you,' she whispered tremulously, her eyes widening as he expelled a long-drawn-out breath.

'Thank heavens for that—perhaps now we can go and have that coffee I went to so much trouble to make.'

Jane drew back from him, unable to believe her ears.

'Stop looking at me like that,' he growled sheepishly. 'I had to say something—didn't I?'

'You did?' she gasped as his hands began moving against her body, making rational thought a virtual impossibility for her.

'You're not the only one who didn't know it was possible to feel this happy,' he told her huskily. 'For one terrible moment I thought you might say no.'

'You did?' she croaked once more, his words

wreaking almost as much havoc on her as his hands as he drew her purposefully back into his arms.

'I did—and, until you're officially my sleeping partner for life, I'm afraid I'm going to keep on experiencing terrible moments like that.'

'It looks as though this marriage is going to have to take place with the utmost haste,' she gasped distractedly as her body began responding with urgent excitement to the familiar magic being wrought on it.

'With the utmost of indecent haste,' he agreed with hoarse ardour, as she drew his head down to hers and began doing with her mouth to his what his hands were doing to her body.

YOU <u>CAN</u> AFFORD THAT HOLIDAY!

Great savings can be made when you book your next holiday – whether you want to go skiing, take a luxury cruise, or lie in the Mediterranean sun – the Holiday Club offers you the chance to receive **FREE HOLIDAY SPENDING MONEY** worth up to 10% of the cost of your holiday!

All you have to do is choose a holiday from one of the major holiday companies including Thomson, Cosmos, Horizon, Cunard, Kuoni, Jetsave and many more.

Just call us* and ask if the holiday company you wish to book with is included.

HOW MUCH SPENDING MONEY WILL I RECEIVE?

The amount you receive is based on the basic price of your holiday. Add up the total cost for all holiday-makers listed on your booking form – excluding surcharges, supplements, insurance, car hire or special excursions where these are not included in the basic cost, and after any special reductions which may be offered on the holiday – then compare the total with the price bands below:-

YOUR TOTAL BASIC HOLIDAY PRICE FOR ALL PASSENGERS	FREE HOLIDAY SPENDING MONEY
£ 200..............449	£ 20
450..............649	30
650..............849	40
850..............1099	60
1100..............1499	80
1500..............1999	110 ...
... 8500 or more	500

Having paid the balance of your holiday 10 weeks prior to travelling, your **FREE HOLIDAY SPENDING MONEY** will be sent to you with your tickets in the form of a cheque from the Holiday Club approximately 7-10 days before departure.

We reserve the right to decline any booking at our discretion. All holidays are subject to availability and the terms and conditions of the tour operators.

HOW TO BOOK

1. CHOOSE YOUR HOLIDAY from one of the major holiday companies brochures, making a note of the flight and hotel codes.

2. PHONE IT THROUGH* with your credit card details for the deposit and insurance premium, or full payment if within 10 weeks of departure and quote P&M Ref: H&C/MBC185. Your holiday must be booked with the Holiday Club before 30.6.92 and taken before 31.12.93.

3. SEND THE BOOKING FORM from the brochure to the address above, marking the top right hand corner of the booking form with P&M Ref: H&C/MBC185.

If you prefer to book by post or wish to pay the deposit by cheque, omit stage 2 and simply mail your booking to us. We will contact you if your holiday is not available.

Send to: The Holiday Club·
P O Box 155 Leicester LE1 9GZ
* Tel No. (0533) 513377
Mon – Fri 9 am – 8 pm, Sat 9 am – 4 pm
Sun and Bank Holidays 10 am – 4 pm

CONDITION OF OFFER

Most people like to take out holiday insurance to cover for loss of possessions or injury. It is a condition of the offer that Page & Moy will arrange suitable insurance for you – further details are available on request. In order to provide comprehensive cover insurance will become payable upon confirmation of your holiday.

Free Holiday Spending Money is not payable if travel on the holiday does not take place.

The Holiday Club is run by Page & Moy Ltd, Britain's largest single location travel agency and a long standing member of ABTA.

N.B. Any contractual arrangements are between yourselves and the tour operators not Mills & Boon Ltd.

ABTA 99529 Page & Moy Ltd Reg No. 1151142

WIN A LUXURY CRUISE

TO THE MEDITERRANEAN AND BLACK SEA

Ever dreamed of lazing away the days on the open sea with all you need to enjoy yourself close at hand, and spending busy, exciting hours ashore exploring romantic old cities and ports?

Imagine gliding across calm blue waters with the sun overhead in a vast blue sky, and waking up in faraway places for breakfast, such as Lisbon with its fashionable shops, or at the famous rock of Gibraltar.

Imagine sailing through the Mediterranean and stopping at Sicily with towering Mt Etna, then arriving effortlessly in Athens with all its many treasures and finally cruising along the Bosphorus and exploring the exotic city of Istanbul.

This experience of a lifetime could be yours, all you need to do is save the red token from the back of this book and collect a blue token from any Mills & Boon Romance featuring the holiday competition in December. Complete the competition entry form and send it in together with the tokens.

Don't miss this opportunity! Watch out for the Competition in next month's books

Accept 4 Free Romances and 2 Free gifts

•FROM READER SERVICE•

An irresistible invitation from Mills & Boon Reader Service. Please accept our offer of 4 free Romances, a CUDDLY TEDDY and a special MYSTERY GIFT... Then, if you choose, go on to enjoy 6 captivating Romances every month for just £1.60 each, postage and packing free. Plus our FREE newsletter with author news, competitions and much more.

Send the coupon below to:
Reader Service, FREEPOST, PO Box 236, Croydon, Surrey CR9 9EL.

- - - - - - - NO STAMP REQUIRED - - - - - - -

Yes! Please rush me my 4 free Romances and 2 free gifts! Please also reserve me a Reader Service Subscription. If I decide to subscribe I can look forward to receiving 6 new Romances each month for just £9.60, postage and packing is free. If I choose not to subscribe I shall write to you within 10 days - I can keep the books and gifts whatever I decide. I may cancel or suspend my subscription at any time. I am over 18 of age.

Name Mrs/Miss/Ms/Mr _____ EP17R

Address _____

_____

Postcode _____ Signature _____

Mills & Boon

Next month's Romances

Each month, you can choose from a world of variety in romance with Mills & Boon. These are the new titles to look out for next month.

THE STONE PRINCESS Robyn Donald

TWO-FACED WOMAN Roberta Leigh

DIAMOND FIRE Anne Mather

THE GOLDEN GREEK Sally Wentworth

SAFETY IN NUMBERS Sandra Field

LEADER OF THE PACK Catherine George

LOVEABLE KATIE LOVEWELL Emma Goldrick

THE TROUBLE WITH LOVE Jessica Hart

A STRANGER'S TRUST Emma Richmond

HIS WOMAN Jessica Steele

SILVER LADY Mary Lyons

RELUCTANT MISTRESS Natalie Fox

SHADOW HEART Cathy Williams

DEVON'S DESIRE Quinn Wilder

TIRED OF KISSING Annabel Murray

WIFE TO CHARLES Sophie Weston

STARSIGN
STARS IN THEIR EYES Lynn Jacobs

Available from Boots, Martins, John Menzies, W.H. Smith and other paperback stockists.

Also available from Mills and Boon Reader Service, P.O. Box 236, Thornton Road, Croydon, Surrey CR9 3RU.